LITTLE AMERICA

Little America

DIANE SIMMONS

 THE OHIO STATE UNIVERSITY PRESS / COLUMBUS

Library of Congress Cataloging-in-Publication Data
Simmons, Diane
  Little America / Diane Simmons.
     p. cm.
  ISBN 978-0-8142-5178-2 (pbk. : alk. paper)—ISBN 978-0-8142-9258-7 (cd-rom)
  1. Short stories, American—21st century. I. Title.

  PS3619.I5584L58 2011
  813'.6—dc22

                              2010054476

Cover design by James A. Baumann
Text design by Juliet Williams
Type set in Adobe Granjon
Printed by The HF Group

♾ The paper used in this publication meets the minimum requirements of the American National
Standard for Information Sciences—Permanence of Paper for Printed Library Materials. ANSI
Z39.48–1992.

9   8   7   6   5   4   3   2   1

To my father, Dale Ellis,
who always looked good in a stockman's hat

Contents

Acknowledgments

Thanks to The Ohio State University MFA Program in Creative Writing and The Ohio State University Press for their sponsorship of The Ohio State University Prize for Short Fiction. Thanks as well to the contest readers for loving short stories enough to plow through a gazillion of them.

My heartfelt gratitude to fellow writers and readers, Roger Wall and Carlos Hernandez, who read most of these stories. Their comments provided much-needed encouragement while simultaneously bringing to light examples of authorial obtuseness. Thanks to the editors who rejected stories with encouraging words and to those who graciously accepted them. Readers and editors at the little magazines are the heroes of literary publishing; they keep us alive. Thanks to the Millay Colony, serene in the snow, where this collection suddenly came into view. As always, thanks to my husband, best friend, and constant supporter, Burt Kimmelman.

Some of these stories have been previously published elsewhere:

"Little America." *Beloit Fiction Journal* 23 (2010).
"Roll." *Oregon Literary Review* 4.2 (2009). http://orelitrev.startlogic.com/
    v4n2/OLR-simmons.htm
"Suitcase*." Blood Orange Review* 4.2 (2009). http://www.bloodorange
    review.com/v4-2/v4-2.htm
"Ticket." *Hamilton Stone Review* 17 (2009). http://hamiltonstone.org/hsr
    17fiction.html#ticket
"Yukon River." *Missouri Review* 33.1 (2010).

Little America

They'd all blow in to some hick town where Hank and Lorraine would put on a program in a hall they'd hired for the night. Gorgeous in aviators and rattlesnake books, Hank jumped and spun and flirted with ladies and men alike as Lorraine chain-smoked and flipped charts that showed how people in other towns had gotten richer and happier and even better-looking since they'd bought whatever it was Hank happened to be selling. When it was over—sometimes even before it was over—they'd jump in the car and speed out of there, driving a hundred miles before stopping to sleep, Hank harmonizing with the radio all the way.

Billie—who spent these evenings watching TV in the motel room if they had one, or reading romance novels in the back of the hall if they didn't—knew they were crooks of some sort. Beyond that, she didn't know much, such as where they came from or what their real names were. Even the idea of a "real name"—as opposed to the name you were using just then—was something she didn't pick up until the third grade when the teacher asked why she had started writing Bunny Miller on her papers instead of Billie Moore.

Billie made a rule for herself then: don't change your name unless you have to. And she kept Billie for many years, even when Hank and Lorraine went to Mel and Monica and then Clark and Inez.

Whatever Hank—as Billie always thought of him—was up to, it required a lot of travel and over the years a variety of cars. A few of them were purring and fragrant; most were banging and stinking of other people's cigarettes or, especially in the backseat where Billie rode, throw-up.

Whatever sort of car it was, the first thing Hank did was install a telescoping rod across the backseat so he could hang up his clothes. Billie rode along back there in a forest of swaying cowboy shirts and fringe-sleeved jackets, all smelling deliciously of Hank's aftershave and sweat.

No matter what had just happened, Hank was always happy driving along. He loved every kind of scenery and was always telling Billie to look out the window to see how the tall grass seemed to be racing away in the wind or how the high mountains looked just exactly like frosted glass. One memorable dawn in Eastern Oregon—up early to beat a wide-awake motel operator and wanting to avoid troopers on Interstate 84—they had headed south from Pendleton on a two-lane road through the wheat fields. As the dawn began to creep over the vast, unbroken fields of ripe wheat, Hank was so overwhelmed he stopped the car. Lorraine wouldn't wake up and look, but Hank and Billie stood by the side of the road for fifteen minutes watching the purple, then pink-soaked wheat turn the purest gold, as far as the eye could see.

"What would you have to pay to see something like that?" Hank asked when they finally got back in the car.

While Hank could be brought almost to tears by the scenery of the West, he had nothing but pity for the squares in the little towns they passed through. His scorn he saved for the men who worked in the stores, men who seemed to think they were something because they stood behind a cash register in a white shirt and a clip-on tie.

Hank had a little more respect for the farmers and ranchers; at least they were out in scenery. Still, when he saw somebody out on a tractor plowing in big slow circles, he would ask, "What could they be *thinking* about all the time?"

Lorraine, who was said to be Billie's mother, spent most of her time smoking and didn't talk much, though Hank, maybe as a joke, said she was the brains of the outfit.

"You can tell she used to be a preacher's wife," Hank would say. Billie was pretty sure *that* was a joke.

Lorraine didn't talk to or look at Billie unnecessarily, and Billie was certain that if she got left behind at a filling station bathroom one day, Lorraine would not be coming back to pick her up. Hank probably would if they remembered in time and weren't like three hundred miles away already.

"Where was I born?" Billie asked Lorraine once when they were alone.

Lorraine blew out a nose full of smoke.

"Montana," she said.

But when Billie asked Hank separately, he answered without hesitation: "Rock Springs, Wyoming. What a pit *that* was."

Of course they never wanted to slip into the habit of telling the truth.

Lorraine and Billie seemed weakly linked, if at all, but Hank and Billie both had the same curly red-orange hair so that waitresses seeing them often said, "I guess I know who your Daddy is!"

Hank was tall and trim, and when he got dressed up, which was most of the time, he looked just like a movie star. No matter what, he had to have good boots and a newish cowboy hat. Just about the only time he really lost his good humor was if somebody disturbed his hat where it rode on the little ledge above the backseat. It had to sit there all alone because if you crowded stuff beside it, the brim would curl up wrong. Then too, during one period when they must have been flush, he got himself a necktie made of real mink. When he took it off, he would wrap it up in an old silk neckerchief, then carefully stuff it inside a cardboard toilet-paper tube.

Besides being good-looking and well-dressed, Hank was also a little bit famous, having once been the object of an investigation by the Idaho attorney general. He'd been in the newspaper for it, and just before they left Idaho and crossed into Wyoming, he'd bought several editions of the paper and then carefully ripped out of each the articles that had his name in it. He folded the articles and put them in his little leather bag of important things.

At one point, waiting alone in a motel room somewhere, Billie had taken the article out and read it but hadn't found out much besides that Hank was selling something he shouldn't.

It was exciting to see his name in print though.

"We don't hurt anybody much," Hank told her after they'd been run out of Idaho. It was the one time they talked about business. "And sometimes we do them some good."

This talk took place in a window booth at truck stop called Little America that they'd reached after a couple of days driving east through Wyoming. They'd been seeing signs for it, practically since Idaho, so many signs, in fact, that Billie figured it would be a big nothing. When they got there, though, it *was* the biggest, fanciest truck stop, surely in the world, with parking for maybe a hundred tractor trailers.

They'd gotten there late and slept in the car—Hank and Lorraine tilted back in the front seats, Billie snuggled amid the bags and bundles in the back. All night they could hear the soothing whine of the high-speed trucks approaching then departing across the flat plain.

Lorraine was still sleeping when Billie and Hank unfolded themselves from the car and went into the fine restaurant there. Hank sat over his tea with lemon, and Billie with a root beer. It was a pink, hopeful dawn and there was a cheerful waitress who winked and slipped Billie a free dough-nut for getting up so early and for having such a good-looking daddy. Bil-lie loved it when waitresses flirted with Hank, because then they almost never ran out on the bill. It was nice to eat without thinking about your exit, even though Hank—who hated paying for things or letting go of his money in any way—would be a little grumpy for half an hour because of it.

"We may not be one hundred percent on the up-and-up," Hank had told Billie as they sat in Little America. "But it's only fraud. And fraud isn't violent."

Hank stopped and looked out over the lines of trucks and the immense blue sky. Billie was a little worried to hear him speak so soberly and won-dered if they were really in trouble. But it seemed it was only the gran-deur of early morning at Little America that had caused him to be so thoughtful.

"I've known violent people," Hank said, "and not one of them could make a plan or talk their way out of a paper bag. Well, I don't have much respect for that type of person. And maybe it isn't nice to say so"—here he paused and looked back into the kitchen where you could see a fat, hairy cook smacking the grill with a giant spatula—"but I think you'll find that violent people are almost always, well, almost always, unattractive to look at."

The next time she found herself in a schoolroom, Billie tried to look up "fraud," but it wasn't, evidently, spelled like it sounded. She knew enough, of course, not to ask the teacher what it meant.

As Billie was in her adolescent years, they seemed to have drifted more to the east, maybe because of being famous in Idaho. The winter she was sixteen, they'd come to perch briefly in Grand Island, Nebraska, waiting out the worst of the cold weather before making one of their big swings down through Kansas, then back up through Colorado and Wyoming.

Hank had found them an old bullet-shaped, thirty-foot trailer in a six-trailer court. It wasn't far from the tracks, and all night long you heard the slow freight trains go clacking past, which was probably why Hank had picked it.

The place was run by an obese and filthy woman named Stella who couldn't stop flirting with Hank.

"I'll get you, boy!" she would yell out the door when he passed by her trailer. "Wait'll I get my teeth!"

Stella ignored Lorraine and Billie, but every day around noon she would come flopping over to their trailer to see Hank. She wore an old bathrobe, obscenely held together over her massive chest with a safety pin, and carried a tin pie plate in her hand.

"Here's your grits, boy!" she'd yell, pounding on their trailer until Hank came out. "Steamin' hot!"

Billie could take the bathrobe and the grits; that was Hank's problem. But she hated the signs Stella had up all over, scrawled on boards in smeary lipstick with a spelling that was completely made up. Some were advertising the trailer court; most were warning trespassers what Stella would do to them if they dared come on her property. There was something terrifying about the bright-red ignorance of those signs. How, Billie wondered, did some little kid end up being Stella?

It was during those winter months that Billie gave up on school and started spending the day at the Grand Island Library reading all the romance novels. It was a cozy place with leather chairs and nice lamps, and the librarian, who admired Billie for coming to Grand Island to help nurse her old aunt, was always looking for new books Billie might like.

It was about this time too that Lorraine kind of disappeared—Hank said something about her visiting family—and in her place there was someone named Pam. Pam talked more than Lorraine and was better-looking, probably, in a plucked sort of way. She also seemed to be a whole lot dumber.

There wasn't any question of whether or not she was Billie's mother which was kind of a relief. In fact, Pam kept trying to make Hank admit that she and Billie looked like sisters.

"I'm closer to her age than yours," she would say to Hank. "We could be your two teenage daughters. Let's watch and see if people take us as sisters."

They didn't look a thing alike, of course, even though Pam's hair was some kind of bottle orange.

When the topic of how Billie and Pam looked like sisters lost its kick, it got replaced by a discussion along the lines of what was Billie going to *do*. It made her wonder what had happened to Lorraine anyway.

Billie had had the odd boyfriend here and there; none of them had done that much for her and she wondered if the whole thing wasn't something mostly made up to sell books. But now, to hedge her bets, she took up with a dark-haired, wet-handed boy named Tom who she met at the library.

Tom was in his second year at the nearby Nazarene College and wanted to become a fourth-grade teacher. He was an anxious, yearning boy who thought Billie was beautiful and who was desperate for sex even though he didn't believe in going all the way until marriage. Around five in the afternoon, he would pick her up at the library where she told him she always went to study after school. They drove out to park at a gravel pit outside of town, and there on the front seat with the heater blasting did everything *but* go all the way until six-thirty when he had to be home for dinner. He would drop her off at a big Victorian house where he thought she lived with that same elderly aunt, and she would walk the fifteen blocks to the trailer court.

Being sex-crazy was one thing about Tom. The other thing about him was his mother, Marge, who was a real mother type with the apron and the stuff cooking and the sewing box with the red tomato pincushion. And who, when she saw Tom coming home all hot and smeary with his shirttail out, quickly found out about Billie and invited her to dinner. She knew Tom was losing his mind over sex and she worried, as she told Billie while they washed up the dinner dishes together, because Tom's other girl friends had been the type of little hot-pants numbers that were bound to keep him from achieving his goals.

"But you seem different," Marge said. "You are so quiet and thoughtful. I always hoped Tom would find a girl like you."

"Well," Billie said. "I guess being an orphan makes you different."

"Maybe you'll be *my* daughter one day," Marge said, looking so frankly and hopefully into Billie's eyes that Billie could not help shuddering slightly. Seeing the shudder, Marge gave Billie a big squeezy hug.

It was only a backup plan, but it's good to plan because one day, sure enough, Billie came home from an afternoon with Tom to find Pam in the back of the trailer packing up, and Hank standing in the trailer's little front room clearing his throat. He said he was glad to see her because he had something for her: two New Mexico driver's licenses, one under the name Billie Moore, and another under the name of Lola Lester. Both put her age at eighteen, which would make her old enough to be on her own.

Hank handed over the I.D., cleared his throat, and looked out the door of the little trailer and finally said that he and Pam had to leave town unexpectedly, and, instead of taking Billie with them, they were planning to put her on a bus to Winnemucca where Hank had heard a young person could get a job in the casinos and do real well. Start off in Winnemucca, Hank advised; then work up to Reno. She should stay away from Las Vegas, though, because Hank had heard it was full of show-offs.

They stood there in the little old trailer house and looked at each other. Hank cleared his throat again.

"You'll make it just fine," Hank said. "Sharp girl like you."

"I'll need a stake," Billie said.

"Oh, well sure," Hank said, shifting around a little and caressing the bills in his pocket. "Sure you will."

"I'll pay you back when I get set up," she said.

They both smiled at this.

They packed the car late that night, using the flashlights they had for such moments even though Stella, who hadn't been paid any rent yet, was always dead drunk by midnight; you could hear her snore all over the court. Still it always felt good to clear out invisibly before daybreak, and they eased past Stella's trailer in first gear. They drove to the Grand Island bus depot, and while Pam waited in a no-parking zone, Hank and Billie went in to buy a ticket to Winnemucca.

Hank said he and Pam would send their new address right away. Billie said she'd send her address too, but of course neither of them would be likely to have an address any time soon and then where would you send it? Looking off in another direction, Hank slid her four fifty-dollar bills and gruffly told her to put it under the insole of her shoe. After she'd done it, he suddenly pulled out one more fifty-dollar bill and put it in her hand.

She knew he hadn't meant to give her the last fifty and for the first time she felt like crying.

"I'll pay you back," she said.

He looked away, cleared his throat a couple of times.

"Oh," he said. "Only if you're flush."

When the eastbound bus pulled in at four-twenty, Hank saw her on, saw her suitcase into the cargo space underneath. Then, from inside the dark, cigarette-and-upholstery-cleaner-smelling bus, she watched him turn and walk away, tall and square shouldered, resetting his hat as he went.

Once he was gone, she got off the bus, got her bag from underneath, and went in to the depot to get the ticket refunded. She sat in the station until daylight, then took the station cab to Tom's house where she told Tom's mother that her aunt had died and another aunt, a mean one, had taken four days off work to drive out from Winnemucca and have a cremation. Now this aunt was going to take Billie back with her and put her to work in the casinos. Of course Marge invited Billie to move right in with them. She put Tom down in the basement for safety, giving Billie his room which was next to Marge's own.

Who knows how this might have turned out if Marge hadn't been quite so determined to love Billie as if she were her own child. But she *was* determined, and it meant that, for one thing, she wanted to share feelings with Billie, to talk about her dear deceased husband and her failure to have a second child. Then too she wanted to talk about Billie's lost parents and the poor deceased aunt. In this way, Marge seemed to think, they would grow close. But Billie didn't know much about sharing feelings unless it was about mountains or dawn or something. Otherwise, feelings had seemed to be something you made up when people seemed to want you to. But while it had been easy enough to make up stuff up to tell people you weren't going to see again, here, stuck with Marge all the time, you had to remember what you'd said in way that was both nerve-wracking and tedious.

The one feeling Billie did have, maybe, was missing Hank. She seemed to miss most of all how the back of his head looked with his hat set at a very slight tilt, and the way he would look up and give her a wink in the rearview mirror. But there wasn't any point in talking to Marge about that. Anyway, Billie was supposed to be an orphan.

It was as much to get away from living with Marge as it was to keep Tom from exploding that Billie agreed to get married. Marge arranged for them to have a little wedding at the justice of the peace. The three of them drove over to his house one evening and made him get up from *Gunsmoke* and go into his little study where he had a desk and a book of wedding certificates. His wife came in as a witness and they stood there and did it, all the time hearing the sound of gunfire coming from the front room.

Then they went back to the little one-bedroom house that Marge had gotten set up for them, stocking it with old sheets and dishes that she'd been saving, and a box of condoms for their bedside table, since they couldn't start a family until Tom graduated.

As far as Tom was concerned, things went pretty well. He was at school or work most of the time, trying to graduate early so he could start supporting a family. He ate his supper while he was at his job as a campus security guard, so there wasn't need for much when he got home late but sex and sleep. He was a boy who tried to do what was expected of him, and if he got to screw every night, things were just fine.

Marge was more complicated, and—as Billie should probably have known—getting married didn't get rid of her. In fact, it made her worse, because now she wanted to help Billie fix up the little house and to teach her the tricks of housekeeping that Billie, as an orphan, had missed out on. In theory Billie liked the idea of a fixed-up house; sometimes in the past she had felt a little jealous when she glimpsed the luxury of other people's lives. In practice, though, a fixed-up house turned out to be way more trouble than it was worth. She was shocked , for instance, to find out what you went through to make and put up curtains in just one room: the measuring, the shopping, the cutting and sewing, the screwing of stuff up to the wall, the standing back to see if it was crooked, the taking it down and putting it up again.

Billie decided the house was fine like it was. It was better than a lot of places.

Like a lot of people who don't want to do housework, she got herself a job, working the lunch shift at a truck-stop restaurant and motel out on the interstate. It's true she couldn't bring herself to show up every day; going every day made you seem like such a suck-up. But her boss, Mr. Rexley, was a nice old man who liked to look at girls with good legs, and who seemed to buy her story about emergencies with a mother who had gone senile.

Billie was surprised to see that having a job wasn't that bad. It was kind of fun, for a change, to be on the other side of the counter and to ironically eye those who came in, as she and Hank had been eyed so many times. Also it was interesting to see that all the waitresses and busboys smuggled out food. That you could be legit and steal at the same time; Billie wondered if Hank had realized such a thing was possible. Of course she liked the tips that nobody reported, that there was no reason for Tom or Marge to know the extent of, and that Billie converted into big bills and stored—along with Hank's fifties—in the sole of her shoe.

In a way, the job was a kind of halfway house between the straight life and the road. It was close enough to the interstate that you could step out the back for a minute, squat down on your heels, lean your back against the cinder-block wall and listen to the whine of the trucks. Then you could go back in and pick up a coffeepot and slide dollar bills into your apron pocket.

And then too there were times when she liked getting back to her own little house after a shift at work. She'd walk the half-mile from the bus stop, let herself in the back door, and sit down in her uniform and coat at the kitchen table, feeling the kind of pleasant tiredness that work could give you. She'd sit eating cold sirloin steak out of the sack she'd smuggled it home in, licking the grease off her fingers, and reading a romance in the pink afternoon light that came in from the west. At such moments she might have said she was happy, and maybe if it could have been like that most of the time, she would have slowly gotten tamed.

But so often there was Marge at the back door, loaded down with shelf paper and paint samples and recipes, looking right in because of course there were no curtains yet.

"Honey," Marge would say, dropping all the stuff on the table. "Turn on the heat when you come home, Dear, and the lights. Take off your coat for goodness' sake. Shall we make some brownies to treat Tom later? I can show you how to make his favorites. Did you shop?"

Marge would open the refrigerator where there might be only a jar of mayonnaise and a petrified lemon.

"Shall we go to Safeway? Next time, though, why not shop the Tuesday specials?"

Marge was determined to be patient and loving. She could understand that someone had never learned how to make a nice home. What she probably couldn't get was that you wouldn't want to learn. And she was no doubt a little scared; the marriage had, after all, been pretty much her idea. So she wasn't about to give up.

Meanwhile Billie did what she'd always done when people got too interested in what was really going on with her, which was to go blank, sometimes sitting with her finger in her book until Marge finally left, close to tears. Then Billie couldn't stand the house. The house was just another version of Marge, wanting every impossible thing from her and never letting her get a minute's peace. Then she would put on her coat to walk to 7-Eleven and shoplift something.

She got so that instead of going home after her shift, she would bribe one of the Mexican chambermaids to let her into an unused room. She would lie carefully on one of the beds and read until it was too late for Marge to come over. Or she would draw a bath and sit in the hot water and not think.

"You like horses?" asked some tall, skinny, cowboy type who'd ordered the Blue Plate Special steak dinner, mashed potato *and* French fries, cherry pie à la mode with an extra scoop.

"No," she said, filling his coffee cup and moving on. You work a truck stop for five minutes and you find out everybody has something cute to say.

"Can you ride?" he asked when she passed back by.

"No," she said.

"Look," he said when she passed by the next time. He glanced out the plate-glass window toward a shiny new pickup truck with a horse trailer hitched to the back. "That's mine."

"Rooty-toot-toot," Billie said.

He laughed at that. She saw that he wasn't that old. Twenty-something, maybe.

"Why don't you come with me up to Montana to a rodeo," he said. "It's a good rodeo. Good purse. I'll win it. I'm a bulldogging champ. I took the grand prize in Nampa. That's how I got my truck. That and another big purse I won down in Utah."

He nodded out the window again toward the shiny truck.

"Come with me," he said. "I could use a girl."

"What for?"

"Girls take your mind off of things," he said. "Keep you from getting too keyed up. The right girl anyhow. Not some Mama's girl. You know."

"I'm married," she said.

She held up her left hand with its thin gold ring.

"Oh yeah? Who too?"

"This kid. He's in college. He's going to be a teacher."

"Teacher, huh? Must be smart. Must be some stud to rate a girl like you."

"He's OK."

Billie went to get a lady's banana cream pie from the pie case. Outside the window the new pickup gleamed. She'd thought it was greenish but really it was more of a midnight blue.

"Only," he said, when she had to pass down the counter again, "Montana is so pretty this time of year. I don't know if you've ever been up there. Probably not, huh?"

"Yeah, I've been up there. I've probably been up there more than you. I'm not *from* here."

"But you're here now. Looks like."

Billie gave him his check. Maybe if he'd walked over to the cashier to pay, that would have been that. Instead he took the check, reset his hat, and walked unhurried past the cashier's stand where Mr. Rexley, his glasses up on his forehead, a rubber tip on his thumb, and a frown on his face, was counting and recounting a pile of singles.

Suitcase

Some people were yelling that it was bourgeois to care if the kitchen floor pulled at your socks. Yeah, and what was wrong with shit on the side of the toilet? Shit's natural.

But other people were yelling just as loud that it was false consciousness—whatever that was—to equate filth with opposition to the status quo.

Marie, who had been in the house only a couple of days, tried to stay out of it by hiding in the curtained-off bay window where they'd said she could sleep. But a big girl in braids and overalls named Sheila came over and yanked the curtain back. This was a collective, she said, and everybody had to participate. It even seemed that Marie's vote was needed to break the tie over whether or not there should be household chores. Some people said she shouldn't be forced to vote, that *that* was bourgeois, and as things went on, they urged her to refuse to vote. The other group agreed that, no, she shouldn't be forced to vote, but that she should *want* to vote and she'd better.

It was 1972, and probably too late to be showing up in San Francisco, but Marie didn't know that. Even if she had known, she would have probably gone anyhow. She had to go somewhere, and San Francisco was in the news, still, as someplace.

Now everyone turned to look at her.

"Well," Marie said. "I mean."

"Oh yeah, she better talk," said Chick, a burly, older guy—thirty, maybe—with an immense, graying ponytail and thick glasses. Because he'd made money on a crab boat in Alaska, he had a big upstairs room to himself and a newish Volkswagen van parked in back. At night on the porch he talked about his plan to drive down to Guatemala and join the Indians in their fight against a repressive government.

Chick had beers that he kept locked in a little fridge up in his room. Every night he went up and got one for him and one for Marie.

"She better talk," Chick said now. "'Cause this is a dictatorship. Want me to get the thumb screws, Sheila?"

"Yeah, Sheila, dig it," said a skinny kid who was called Spider.

"What, she needs big strong men to defend her?" yelled Sheila's friend, Rose, another big girl in overalls. "She needs some big phony bullshit supposed-to-be revolutionary and some little, some little . . . ."

Rose couldn't think of anything bad enough to call Spider, but already Sheila and a couple of other girls had picked up a familiar thread, yelling that the men in the house were every bit as sexist as their lawyer fathers, their banker and oligarch fathers who, at least, weren't hypocrites. Marie didn't know what an oligarch was. She was impressed, though, if their fathers were really bankers and lawyers.

Now everyone started yelling, "Fuck you!" Some of the girls were crying and some of the guys were laughing and saying how predictable, how too, too predictable.

The next day Marie moved upstairs with Chick, and within a week they were driving south on I-5 in Chick's van. They drove out of the wet, soft air and low, purple sky of the north, and into the clear day of Southern California, heading toward Nogales where they would cross into Mexico and then drive south to Guatemala.

They didn't have to stop at motels because Chick had spent about a year getting the van rigged up to live in. They slept in sleeping bags on a foam pad that was cut to fit the van's floor; when the pad wasn't in use, it fit neatly along one wall. Dishes and cooking gear were stowed in a special wooden box that could open out into a work space.

Chick taught Marie how to use the various pieces of gear—the folding grill, the Dutch oven, the reflector oven—to cook over a fire at the campsites where they stopped. Once you got the hang of it, it wasn't that hard. Marie had done all the cooking at home since she was nine, and she could probably cook upside down if it came to that.

Chick had grown up half-blind in a waterlogged little town on the Oregon coast with a teenage mother and a series of fathers, some better than others. He'd started turning gray at age twelve. Once he'd gotten old enough to be on his own, he was determined to rely only on himself for everything. That was why he'd fixed up the van with everything you would need, and why he would not think of staying in a smoke-stinking motel or of eating the un-nutritious food found in restaurants. He would rather stop and walk off into a field than use the foul bathrooms of a service station.

Another result of Chick's childhood was that he felt really sorry for people. That was probably what got Marie on board, at least in part. His poor, barely-seeing eyes behind their magnifying lenses filled with tears to think of her growing up on a dry little Nebraska Sand Hills farm, the lonely child of a wordless, endlessly working father and a mother who had lost track of everything but the time and even *that* she had to check three or four times a minute on a man's big watch.

Chick felt so sorry for little Marie, alone on that silent farm, that he wanted to do everything for her. Before leaving San Francisco, he had taken her to get birth control pills and wept when they first had sex. With his glasses off he looked at her with his nearly blind eyes and said that he wanted to take care of her forever. Marie didn't know about forever. But it was nice to be taken care of.

When they made Nogales, they paid a daily rate in a trailer park so they could use the laundry room and have a place to spread out and organize the supplies they were loading up for the trip down to Guatemala. They went to a hippie food co-op for the health food supplies Chick used, packages of soy nut cereals, and cans of food yeast to supply the B vitamins most people didn't get. At a regular grocery store they loaded up on dried milk and peanut butter, which Chick had heard was an expensive delicacy in Mexico. They got a half-gallon of Clorox and some eyedroppers that they would use to purify water.

Marie got Chick to stop at a paperback exchange where she bought a bunch of ragged mysteries, even though Chick didn't approve of the crap they made up for books. But he was happy, at least at first, when she found a book that taught you to speak Spanish; they started to study from it so they could talk to the Indians they were going to be fighting alongside. For a few nights they tried to piece together some phrases, like "We are here to obey you." But after a couple of nights Chick remembered that Spanish was the language of the oppressor as much as English. They should learn, he said, Mayan, or whatever the people in Guatemala really spoke. So that was it for Spanish.

The real Mexico didn't look much like the pictures of senoritas and bull-fighters in the *Learn Spanish* book. At first, there was nothing but the road, cratered and surfaceless and traveled only by a few ancient trucks with their high, drooping loads, meandering along at fifteen miles an hour. For the first time in her life, Marie considered the beauty of the shining black American interstate, of the new and speeding cars, and the great, scream-ing tractor trailers.

But Chick was teary-eyed with joy when, on their second night, they found their way off the road and onto the dead-fish-stinking beach at Topolobampo. He wept because they had escaped the criminal material-ism, the mind-fucking lies, and the unnatural stink of America, a stink that was, he taught, a lot worse than the natural and wholesome smell of decomposing flesh.

They drove south and south, avoiding cities and large towns where Chick was afraid they would see the putrid American influence. As they drove, Chick talked about why they had to go fight in Guatemala. He pounded the steering wheel about United Fruit and the CIA who had brought down a government that was trying to help the poor people. The massa-cres, Chick cried. The death squads. The illiteracy. The more-or-less slav-ery. All these crimes at America's more-or-less door.

Marie learned never to smile when he was talking. Once she must have because he yelled, "It's no joke, Baby!"

Outside the van, the world swam by, hot and green now, restfully pointless, and if she had thought about it she would have said that she didn't believe they were going to fight for the Indians any more than she had believed her mother ever knew what time it was.

Here, there were more people, or maybe people were just out more than they were in the dead, dry North. Men in broad hats, stooping in the wavering green fields, always straightened to stare as the van went past. Old women and little girls walked along the roads with bundles of sticks on their backs. Chick, who looked more and more like a great white bear every day compared to the small, dark Mexicans, tried to offer the old women rides, but they sank terrified back into bushes.

The roads didn't improve but you grew accustomed to them as the idea of speed faded. Maria didn't know what had become of the toilets with their litter of used tissue paper that had so disgusted her at first; she didn't look for them anymore but just plunged into the brush as Chick did. He was as proud when she came out, stepping high and watchful of snakes, as if she had just spoken her first word.

They slept in the van, sometimes with the double doors open to get the breeze that ruffled the mosquito-net curtain Chick had rigged. Once, as they slept, hands reached in over Chick's feet. Marie felt a grip on her ankle and screamed. Chick jumped out, naked and roaring so that Marie laughed.

Chick didn't blame the thieves; they naturally mistook him for a rich American. He only hoped he would have the nerve to rob Americans if he were in their place. In the next town, Chick meekly replaced the tire pump somebody had apparently stolen before reaching into the van.

When they couldn't find a camping place, they grudgingly parked on the *zocalo* of a small town, closing the double van doors and pulling the green canvas curtains Chick had installed for this eventuality. Then they lay in the hot dark—Marie reading by flashlight; Chick with his hands meditatively behind his head—until the town kids stopped pounding on the van and shouting "heepie!" and went home to bed.

When they saw a stream, they clambered down to bathe, though with their clothes on so as not to offend the women who were usually there if the bank was halfway accessible. While the women talked their mile-a-minute Spanish, they slapped clothes on the rocks and hung them on bushes. Though Chick and Marie tried so hard to be polite and respect-ful, the women still didn't want them there, made shooing gestures and shouted phrases that Chick and Marie couldn't understand but that raised a shout of laughter from the others. Chick smiled and made bow-ing motions toward them. Later, driving away, he would wipe tears from under his thick glasses.

He was crying a lot now, Marie noticed.

Sometimes Marie tried to wash their clothes in the river, wrestling with the leaden, water-logged jeans that were as heavy and unwilling as a drowned body. She rubbed in bar soap like the women did, then, uncer-tain as to why, smacked the pants legs on the rocks. Meanwhile a crowd of squatting children watched, commenting softly to one another.

At outdoor markets, where they were followed by crowds of kids, they augmented their supplies with tomatoes and oranges, tasteless white farm-er's cheese, eggs, rum, and any other foods cheap enough that common people could afford them too.

Every meal was cooked over a fire, usually before a silent audience of local children and a few adults who stood in a half-circle, their faces shining in the firelight, staring as if at a fascinating performance. At first Chick had tried to share, had offered to divide the whole pan of food among them, but nobody ventured near the portions he set out in pans and cups.

Chick understood. He understood how they saw him, a rich gringo oppressor. He aligned himself with their distrust of what he represented. He would wait humbly until they could understand and love him as a comrade.

Still he suffered. He would sit with his great white head in his hands, drinking cup after cup of rum and grieving that he could not find a way to show the people how much he loved them, show how much he hated who they thought he was. Who he maybe *was* even.

At first, it seemed that everybody else who'd come to Mexico had done it for the dope. Every market seemed to have a bunch of hippies straggling through, giggling and trailing that particular dirty-clothes-and-pot smell. In some towns every little kid wanted to sell you grass and older guys eyed you appraisingly. Once, as they crossed the zocalo in Culiacan, a band of little boys swarmed around them chirping, "You want money? Big money? Boss says drink beer."

They gestured to a café table on the shady side of the square where a man in a big cowboy hat and sunglasses watched.

Chick was so humiliated that all Americans were expected to treat impoverished Mexico as some kind of opium den that the next day he carried his modest stash of weed out into a field. He took a dump and then buried the dope in the hole with his shit.

But farther south the type of gringo on the road seemed to change. Now the people they met were often on some kind of mission themselves. As they pulled up to camp beside a stream not far from Puebla, they met evangelists, a married couple in their thirties, both tall and blond and bony. Both came hurrying out when Marie and Chick drove into the clearing, both talking at once, her talking into Marie's window and him talking into Chick's. Marie made out that they had just opened a canned chicken they had packed back home in Gallup for some special occasion. Tonight wasn't any special occasion; they'd just gotten to obsessing about that canned chicken. They knew they ought to have waited for a real occa-

sion but the woman—her name seemed to be Honey—had said the Lord
would *send* an occasion, and her husband—they never got his name—had
trusted in that and thought it was right that they trust in it, and that they
shouldn't be so prideful as to think they could make all the decisions their
own small selves. And now here *they* were—Marie and Chick—so that
proved it. It *was* a special occasion. And Chick and Marie had to just come
and sit right down, they had the chicken all ready, cooked in a stew; they
had Bisquick dumplings just coming done on top and they even had gone
into the canned pickled beets. And now that Chick and Maria were so
miraculously here, Honey was just going to root up her own homemade
fruitcake she had hidden away.

Come *on*," Honey said, reaching inside the window and grabbing
Marie's arm. "Oh, praise the Lord for sending me a girl to talk to, and
you're nice, I see you're nice, my Lord, you look so clean, and I feel like a
mess. Goodness, I never knew it would take this much just to *get* there; oh
well, let's just talk about stuff!"

He, meanwhile—the guy—was trying to tell Chick about the indus-
trial-size sewing machine they had in the back of their blue panel truck,
how they were heading down to an evangelical mission near Guatemala
City to set up a little shop, maybe you could call it a little factory, where
the people could sew clothes for themselves, and maybe export things and
the people could be brought to Christ that way because of course the Cath-
olics had gone in there to mix their mumbo-jumbo in with Indian stuff,
and, frankly, once you learned what was going on down there, the Lord
just wouldn't let you off the hook.

Marie, by this time, knew—or should have known anyhow—all about
the Christian evangelists in Guatemala. How they were welcomed by the
killer right-wing government, how they were a symptom of American
anti-communist hysteria, and how they were as key to the oppression of
the people as the thugs with guns.

So she should not have been too surprised when Chick slammed into
reverse, even though these two were still standing there talking, their arms
half inside the van. Tears were streaming down from inside Chick's glasses
as he drove away.

Marie felt like crying too, she'd wanted that chicken dinner so bad.

On another stream, stumbling down the bank with a pan full of dirty dishes,
Marie saw a man standing in thigh-high water. He was a gringo, obviously,
tall and beautiful, bathing naked, his head afluff in shampoo suds.

Afterward he sat on a rock and combed his long blonde hair. He told Marie, who went ahead and squatted by the water with her dishes, that he was on his way to Colombia to do cocaine for a year or two. Then, he said, shrugging sweetly, knowing of course how beautiful he was, he would see. Maybe he would go to New York and become a model. Up above, Chick was watching, looking more white-bear-like than ever.

"Have tea with me," the man said. His name was Laurence; anyway that was what he had stenciled in purple lowercase letters on the side of his camper. The doors were open to show the floor and walls, covered with leopard skin carpeting.

"I have lemon, ginger, and Red Zinger," he said.

Chick of course said no.

And then, while they were camping on a vacant lot on the outskirts of Miniatitlán, another rig pulled up beside them. In it was a gray-haired German man, maybe forty-five or even fifty, driving a new, fitted-out VW van with the pop-up top and the little red leather benches and built-in table. Once he'd gotten settled with his top popped, he came over and invited them in his bad English to come and listen to his short-wave radio. He would make coffee. He had canned milk, he said, for the coffee.

Chick said no. When the guy had gone, Chick explained that a German that age was sure to have been a Nazi. He'd probably driven up from South America where it was well-known they were still hiding.

"Where in South America?" Marie asked.

Chick said it didn't matter.

"Like Bolivia?"

"It doesn't matter. What does it matter if he's a Nazi?"

Later, when Chick went off into the bushes to do some business or other, Marie went over to the German's van. She sat at his little table and took one of his china cups, feeling its creamy smoothness in her hand. She put a lot of the canned milk in her coffee.

The German tuned in his radio to an English station and they listened to a report about a cricket game that was being rained out. This made the German laugh. While they were listening, Chick came pounding on the side of the van, making the German jump and crash his head on the lantern that hung over the table.

After the thing with the German, Chick pretty much stopped talking and they trundled along in silence. Marie avoided looking at the tears that leaked from under his glasses. At night he got stoned on the grass that he'd apparently resupplied himself with; once he was good and stoned, he would lie down in the van and start drinking rum.

What about the Indians, Marie wondered.

One late afternoon they pulled into a clearing outside the ruins of a Mayan temple, Palenque. A couple of weeks earlier Chick would not have dreamed of stopping in a place like this. The clearing was filled with hippie rigs. Everybody was stoned. Everybody was filthy. Everybody was sick with the runs, and the jungle behind the campsite was slick with shit.

Marie thought maybe Chick was trying to get even with her, showing her what happened when you didn't care if people were Nazis or not. She hoped it was that, kind of, and not that Chick was losing it.

Everybody camped in the clearing was talking about how some girl had died a few days ago; the Mexican police came and took her body and her boyfriend. Nobody knew where. Now another girl was sick with more than just the runs. This one was traveling with a guy in a big black Cadillac; they had taken the backseat out and replaced it with a mattress. Everybody knew she was sick but nobody did anything. Everybody was too scared of the cops coming back.

In the day it was hot and quiet, a few cars passing on the dry, white road to the ruins. At night they were alone in the clearing, the jungle buzzing, loud and insane.

The second or third night, a boy and a girl came by the van. The double doors were open; inside Chick snored behind the mosquito-net curtain, already stoned and drunk. Marie was sitting in the cab with a candle, trying to read.

"What luxury," the girl said, looking inside.

The girl was wearing motorcycle boots and a white Mayan dress that came to her knees. The boy was barefoot in a crusty pair of jeans and a T-shirt that had lost most of its back. They squatted down and told a complicated story of how they'd bought an expensive five-pound Dutch cheese at the duty-free port of Chetumal. They had planned to live on it for a long time. But some people picked them up hitchhiking and the people's dog ate their whole cheese. Then, when they got mad about their cheese, the people drove off with all their stuff, what was left of their money and even their shoes. So they'd had to steal the boots off a guy sleeping on his motorcycle and they took turns wearing them. They were sorry—

especially since it was a black guy—but he had wheels so it was kind of fair.

They had a little sack of beans some Mexicans had given them, but nothing to cook them in and no matches. Marie gave them a dozen matches and one of Chick's pots; she told them they would have to build their fire somewhere else though.

"Let's get out of here," Marie said to Chick. "Everybody's sick. We'll catch something."

Chick was lying down in back stoned.

"I can't find the keys," he said.

Walking out into the jungle, going far to find a clean place to pee, Marie came across what looked like a pile of garbage. It wasn't the usual Mexican garbage of a few rotting fruit rinds, but expensive, American-type garbage, papers and books and bottles of things that came from a drugstore. There was a new-looking American Tourister suitcase tossed to the side, and Marie realized that somebody had probably stolen the suitcase, gone through it for money or jewelry, and dumped it.

The thieves hadn't wanted clothes, even though there were nice ones, girl clothes, just a little gooey now with spilled shampoo. Marie combed out of the mess two good, clean pair of underpants. There was a silky, copper-colored shirt, and a good pair of jeans.

There was a pair of baby-doll pajamas dotted with little roses.

Marie held them up, amazed. What kind of a girl would still have baby-doll pajamas?

Standing on the bare jungle floor with the trees arching high above, Marie shucked off her own grimy, smoke-and-dope-and-weeks-of-sweat-smelling pants. She stripped out of her shirt and underwear and left them on the ground; maybe they would be found by someone who would know how to get them clean. She pulled on the new underpants, the copper shirt, and the jeans, which fit perfectly.

She kicked around some more, saw a book and picked it up. It was thick but only a dictionary of some sort; as she tossed it away, a pale blue envelope flew out. Marie put the envelope in her back pocket, then picked the book up and shook it; a green American passport dropped to the ground.

Marie picked it up and studied the picture of a round-faced girl in round, dark-rimmed glasses. She had a brown ponytail and bangs. Gillian, her name was.

Marie looked around for the glasses and there they were, lying in the dirt a few feet away, not broken at all.

She put the passport in her back pocket along with the letter. She put on the glasses and looked into the distance. It seemed like she could see better.

For the first time she thought to look around, but nobody was watching. She started back to the bus before remembering and turning back to find a bush and pee. Only then did she see the girl. Probably. If it was her. If it was, it was too late. So Marie turned and ran.

She didn't tell Chick about the girl or the things she'd found; he didn't wake up enough notice the new clothes or the glasses.

That night, as Chick slept, she climbed up to the cab, sticking a knobby Mexican candle on the dashboard. She leaned against the door, her pillow behind her back. Carefully she unfolded the letter. It was from Gillian's mother.

They all missed her a lot, the mother wrote, especially Jack, who had started jumping up and barking like crazy every time someone came to the door. *They* missed her too, but they were fine. Sue was busy with swim team and Dad was usually able to leave work a little early so he could get home in time to go to the meets. Afterwards Sue was always famished but it seemed too late to cook so they just went to the Italian place in town. Once, at another table, they saw a girl in a ponytail and round-rimmed glasses who, for a second, they all three thought was Gillian.

"We miss you, love," the mother wrote. "But we know you are having fine adventures and learning loads at the language institute. How much you'll have to tell!"

Marie folded up the letter and put it in her pocket with the passport, blew out the candle, and sat for a long time with her back to the door, her feet stretched out under the steering wheel. Outside the van the jungle buzzed so loud it seemed the world was burning.

Holy Sisters

Driving north in a stolen Mustang that is too new and too bright blue.

But there it had been in front of the hotel, the windows open and the key in the ignition, a rabbit's-foot key chain dangling down, so sweet.

Keep walking, I said. And I did, all around the plaza. I must have looked inside thirty cars, most of them clunkers. Not a key in sight.

It was early evening in Merida. The air was warm as a hot tub, and the plaza was full of dressed-up locals: women in those embroidered white dresses, men in loose white shirts. Little kids running and screaming. There was music and some of the old people were dancing. Maybe it was Sunday or something.

All around the plaza were big, smooth trees, the trunks whitewashed shoulder high so that they gleamed in the last of the light. Up there somewhere in the branches was the balcony where we'd sat. Up there with our expensive drinks, breathing in the heavenly smells rising from the food wagons in the plaza below.

I don't know if he ran out of money or if he had a wife somewhere or what. Who knows how Mexicans do these things. I've probably been here long enough anyway. Kevin and those other Phoenix guys have probably forgotten all about me. Guys like that can't remember things for very long.

Now I'm driving back north to the border. I've got about thirty bucks in my pocket and I'm wondering how far that will go on gas. What's the mileage on this thing anyhow? What could I get for the car, I'm wondering, hot though it is. Does *hot* work the same down here?

By two the next afternoon I'm nearing Puebla; the road has gotten wider and smoother and there are more newish cars so I don't stand out so bad. I'm starting to feel pretty good when an unmarked white sedan pulls up beside me. It runs parallel long enough that I can see both guys in it are waving pistols and pointing for me to pull over by the side of the road.

My first thought is that maybe these are Kevin's guys down from Phoenix. Maybe they're smarter than I thought. But no, these are Mexicans and way classier than anybody Kevin would know.

There seems to be a boss, skinny, caramel-colored, reasonable looking. He could have been the manager of a 7-Eleven in El Paso. He smiles and shrugs as if to say sorry about all this. The other guy is big and dark and scary. Both are wearing slacks with ironed, open-collar shirts. Some upscale type of cop maybe, undercover *federales* even. Or maybe some big deal car theft unit.

If they *are* cops. They didn't show badges, and they don't seem to be interested in papers or anything.

Instead they want me to open the trunk.

I get out and walk to the back of the car. I realize as I'm walking that there could be just about anything in that trunk. I'm scared and embarrassed both. Likely those keys were left dangling for some chump to come along and drive it away.

I'm just glad my dad isn't here to see this. My dad—say he happened to be stealing a car—would have opened that trunk first thing. He'd be disgusted at me right now.

But the trunk, which is surprisingly big for such a small car and carpeted in unstained sky blue, is completely empty.

The big guy stands for a second; he's staring into the trunk like if he looks long enough something will pop up. The boss says something and the other guy seems to get furious and starts yelling some rat-a-tat stuff, waving his huge hands around. The big guy has started sweating, and the white shirt that looked crisp a minute ago already has a wet, plate-sized spot on the chest.

The boss keeps talking to the big guy in a quiet, reasonable-sounding voice as if trying to calm him down; at the same time, he's shrugging toward me like, geez, what can you do with a guy like this?

But the big guy doesn't calm down. Still talking mile-a-minute Spanish, he puts his gun in his waistband, pulls out a knife, and then folds himself into the backseat of the Mustang. He reaches up and starts slashing the silky blue lining of the car's ceiling. Meanwhile the boss is making gestures to me like, wow, sorry, I apologize for my friend, what's up with him anyway?

I start crying a little bit. Sometimes it helps.

All that happens now is that the boss snaps something to the other guy that could have been: Now look what you've done. The big guy doesn't answer and doesn't look my way.

"Ta da DA! Ta da DA!" he keeps yelling.

He climbs out of the backseat and sits down in front on the passenger side. He slashes the ceiling lining there too, so it hangs down in ribbons. It's like somebody has decorated the inside of the car for a dance.

The big guy knifes all the seats and the armrests, feels up under the dashboard, then turns on his back, his long legs dangling out the door, to look up under the dash with a little flashlight, but no luck.

He gets out and walks to the front, lifts the hood and looks all around in there but doesn't seem to find anything. He goes over to his car and comes back with a crowbar. He pries off all the hubcaps; they clatter onto the hot road and go rolling into the weeds.

There doesn't seem to be anything under the hubcaps though. The big guy comes back to the trunk again, climbs in, and starts kicking through to the backseat. Then he crawls headfirst from the trunk into to the backseat. It looks like the car has finally decided to eat him.

The boss keeps shrugging like, so sorry, wow, I just don't get it. He's the good cop probably. Or the good drug boss. Or whatever these guys are.

The big guy comes back out of the trunk, then rolls on the ground under the Mustang with his flashlight, looking, apparently, for something stuck to the bottom of the chassis.

"Ta, da DA," he yells out once in a while.

Finally there is nothing in the car left to rip up or poke into. The boss gets back in his car, still holding up his hand to show how puzzled and sorry he is. The other guy, his shirt soaked with sweat, his shirt tail flapping out around his big brown belly, rolls out from under the car and gets in the passenger side. They drive away.

Now I'm scared of the Mustang; maybe somebody else is looking for it. It still starts up so I drive on into Puebla. I drive around until I find the market, then park in a big lot of pounded dirt beside the beat-up rigs people have driven in from the country. The skinny men who are already starting to load up their burlap sacks of unsold vegetables all stop to stare at the car. It still looks pretty OK from the outside, except for the missing hubcaps. I'm thinking, maybe I could find somebody to give me a hundred dollars for it. That would probably get me back up to El Paso.

I'm wandering around the market, not sure what I'm looking for, exactly; somebody who looks like they've got a hundred dollars, I guess.

I'm walking along, past the usual market women squatted over their little piles of brown oranges and doll-sized bananas, when I see an American girl standing up against a hot wall, looking off into space, tears sliding down her face. I stop in front of her, but she doesn't seem to see, just stands there, her fists clenched at her side. She could be stoned, but stoned people don't usually cry.

"What's wrong," I ask her.

"My glasses got stolen," the girl says, looking in my direction. "I can't see. Without them I can't see anything. I can't find my boyfriend. I'm afraid maybe he left. Who are you?"

"A girl, Billie. From the States. How'd they get stolen?"

"I was sitting down waiting for my boyfriend and I went to sleep for a minute."

The girl is looking off into space like Helen Keller.

"My glasses were sitting on top of my pack," she says. "They took my glasses and they took my pack too."

She scrubs her face with her fist.

"So you don't have anything?"

"I have some money sewed in my bra. But I can't see to go anywhere. I'm like blind."

I look around the market. Nearby a woman in a straw hat, more important than the others, sits on a stool to supervise five or six squat burlap bags, each filled to the top with gleaming black coffee beans. She is watching the girl and me to see what will happen next.

The girl and I agree to team up. Her name is Toola and she's from Denver; if I kick in my thirty, she has enough money to buy us both bus tickets to El Paso. My part of the deal will be to guide her around.

I decide to forget about the Mustang; let somebody hotwire it and take their chances.

All Toola can think about is going to a real, American optometrist and getting new glasses. Once she has glasses she'll call her parents and see if they'll still speak to her. Her dad will, she thinks. Her mom, probably not right away. But she knows her mom will lock herself in the bathroom and cry when she hears Toola is OK and coming home.

"He wasn't really my boyfriend," Toola says when we are finally on a bus heading north. It is the usual stinking bus, jammed with silent, suffering Mexicans and a couple of stoned Australian backpackers. It's about a hundred degrees, but there's no air conditioning and the windows don't open.

We all sit quietly, trying to breathe. We can't be going more than thirty miles an hour.

"We were just traveling together," Toola says. "We didn't even have sex. I know that's embarrassing to say."

"Oh, well."

"I'm only eighteen," she says.

"Oh."

"How old are you?"

"Twenty-four."

"Maybe he couldn't find me either. He's probably scared to death now."

"Probably."

"I had a real boyfriend in high school. He was nice. His ears stuck out and turned bright red over almost anything. But really he was nice. He went to college to be an engineer. He probably has a girlfriend by now."

I close my eyes and try to sleep.

"Are you here all alone?" Toola asks.

"Yeah," I say.

"Are your parents furious?"

"No."

"Do they know where you are?"

"I don't know where *they* are," I say. Just to get her to shut up. I never actually knew my mom. I guess she could be floating around out there somewhere. I don't see the point of telling my whole life story though.

After we've been riding a day or so, the girl says, "My name isn't really Toola. It's Mary Anne. I got the name Toola from a dream when I dropped acid. If I can just get home, I'm going back to Mary Anne. Do you think I look more like a Mary Anne than a Toola?"

"Maybe."

"Yes," the girl says. "I know I do. I don't care."

We ride and ride. I imagine going down into a cool, dry cellar that smells like mice and apples. Or I put myself sledding down an endless mountain slope under a cold gray sky.

"I used to want to be a fourth-grade teacher," Mary Anne says. "It's not too late probably. I bet my parent will still let me go to college. My dad will I know."

"Sure."

"What do you want to do?" she asks me.

"Maybe have my own business," I say, just to make something up. I don't know what I'll end up doing. I used to think I would just glide along like my dad, never getting tied down, seeing lots of stuff; a little crooked but not too bad. Not what you'd call really harmful. I'm starting to worry I'm not smart enough though.

"What kind of business?"

"Christ, Mary Anne. I don't know. Something that lets you travel I guess."

"I hate traveling," Mary Anne says. "You can have it."

After a couple of hundred years, we make Chihuahua early one morning. The bus stops at a little plaza on the outskirts of town. We all get off and try to find a place to go to the bathroom or get some food. Mary Anne and I are hungry but we don't have much money left. With her holding my arm, we cross the street to where we can get a stack of tortillas for a couple of pesos. They are warm and good-smelling but don't go far to fill you up. We get one lukewarm Pepsi to share. We stand there and drink, then give back the bottle.

We cross back to the plaza. Over on the shady side a man is sitting at a table. He's wearing a cowboy hat and is carrying a big belly in a dingy white shirt.

He beckons to us. We go over there, Mary Anne hanging on my arm.

"I invite you to a beer, young ladies," he says, smiling in a careful, older guy way.

"Gracias," I say.

"Let's not miss the bus," Mary Anne says.

"It's sitting right there," I say. "I can see when the driver comes back."

I sit down at the table and of course Mary Anne has to sit down too; the man orders us both tall, cold, delicious beers that we slug out of the bottle. It's the first cold thing we've come across for days.

"Muchas gracias," we both say.

"It is nothing," the man says in English.

"You are American young ladies?" the man says.

"Yes," I say.

"Is the bus still there?" Mary Anne asks.

"Yes, right there."

"Can you drive a car, young lady?" the man asks me.

"Sure."

"I have a little truck. This little truck must go to El Paso."

"Oh yeah? What's in the truck?"

"It is the little truck of holy sisters," the man says, smiling. "They are going to El Paso each month. Then they are returning to here with food and clothing and medicines for a mission to los indios Tarahumara in the mountains. It is only one day to here from El Paso. Then the next day, four hours from Chihuahua up into the mountains to the mission. It is so beautiful at the mission. Los indios come there and the sisters help them. They take care of the sick ones and help the old ones. It is like a little heaven there."

"Why don't the sisters drive themselves?"

The man smiled.

"The holy sisters do not learn to drive. So I must get a driver for them. I am the uncle of one of the holy sisters and so I try to help with these things. I like better a lady than a man to drive the holy sisters, understand?"

"I want to get on the bus now," Mary Anne says.

"It's sitting right there," I tell her. "Can't you see that big gray blob? Relax."

Mary Anne starts to cry a little.

"How much are you paying?" I ask the man.

"One hundred dollars each way. Plus you stay at the convent in El Paso for free. When you return, you stay in the mission as long as you wish. The mission is very beautiful, so cool in the mountains. Such beautiful air. It is like perfume."

He stops and takes a deep breath, as if smelling the air now.

"Can you believe, you will want a little fire in your room? Yes, you will have your own little room at the mission. It is simple but so clean and white."

He considers us, smiling.

"Yes, it is like heaven there."

"One-fifty each way," I tell him.

"No," Mary Anne wails. "You promised. I bought your ticket and you promised to help me until we got back."

"My friend has to go with me," I tell the man. "Is there room for her and the nuns too? How many nuns are there?"

"Two only. Two little holy sisters. Yes, of course, your poor friend must go."

"I want to go on the bus," Mary Anne says. "Please let's just get back on the bus. We'll be there in two days."

"Look. Why get back on that awful bus? If we drive, we can get there tonight. Wouldn't you like to get there tonight? Besides, we'll have a place to stay in El Paso. Then tomorrow I can borrow their truck and drive you to get your glasses. Wouldn't that be better? And we'll have money. We can eat. Aren't you hungry? I'm starving."

The man listens, nodding.

Mary Anne lifts her head at the sound of the bus pulling away.

We walk over to the little beat-up Datsun pickup that is sitting right there on the street. I get down and feel up under the dashboard and look under the seats. I roll under and look up at the chassis. There aren't any hubcaps to pry off.

The uncle of the nun is watching.

"All in Mexico are selling drugs?" he asks, smiling.

"No offense. It's just that there was this other car."

"This other car had drugs?"

"No. Some people just thought so."

The man nods.

"Yes, people are always thinking so."

I don't see anything funny-looking and get up off the ground.

"OK. Deal."

The man reaches in his pocket and comes up with one hundred and fifty dollars in a bunch of rumpled twenties, tens, a few ones and some Mexican money. He says I'll get the other one-fifty when I've delivered the nuns and the load of food and clothing up to the mission.

Then he writes out on a piece of paper the address of the convent in El Paso where the food and clothing is collected and where I can stay if I want until it's time to drive back down to Mexico. On the back of the paper, he draws a map for getting from Chihuahua to the mission.

While we are busy with money and directions, two little nuns in black gowns and veils come tiptoeing out from somewhere. The man rattles out something and they climb up in the back of the pickup; they sit with their backs against the window, their little legs in black stockings and lace-up shoes sticking straight out.

They are cute little nuns; they look about thirteen, their faces round and blank. Or they could be thirty-five and just innocent. It's hard to tell with nuns.

"You see, there is space in front for your friend," the guy says.

"You're sure they're OK back there?"

"Oh yes. It is better for them there."

I take Mary Anne's arm and get her into the cab of the pickup. Then I go over to a street wagon and get big plates of beans and chicken and rice for me and Mary Anne; just to be polite I get some for the nuns too and they don't seem to mind. We all sit in the pickup and eat. When we finish, I take the plates back to the street wagon, and we take off north.

How good it feels to drive a car you didn't steal.

How good it feels to have a stomach full of food.

How good the little breeze, flowing through the cab.

"Come on," I say to Mary Anne. "Isn't this better."

"I guess," Mary Anne says. "I just want to get there so bad."

I drive as fast as I can and still not hit a pothole and break the axle.

In back the little nuns in their flowing black garbs are buffeted by the wind. Every so often one of the veils escapes and goes flaring up in the air like a huge soaring bird, swooping over the truck.

"Can you imagine it being cold enough to build a fire?" I say to Mary Anne. "I bet they burn juniper up there. That's why he says it smells like perfume. Have you ever smelled juniper burning?"

Mary Anne says she hasn't.

"It's about the best smell in the world."

"Oh."

"Yeah. I remember once when I was a kid. My dad got his hands on a cabin up in the mountains for a week. I'm not sure where it was exactly. New Mexico maybe. We burned juniper there. You'd never forget the smell. We holed up there a whole week. Just keeping the fire going, shooting the breeze. Hiding out from something I guess. I was just a kid."

Mary Anne says it sounds nice. She says maybe my dad and I can go there again someday.

"Yeah. Well. Probably not."

We stop once at a little roadside joint. The little sisters climb down and we all take turns going around back to pee. I buy everybody cokes. We drink them down and give back the bottles.

"OK?" I ask the sisters. "OK back there?"

They nod up and down, their round little eyes never blinking. They don't look scared at all. They probably trust everybody.

"That mission," I ask them. "Up in mountains? Muy bueno? Muy hermoso?"

The sisters both nod some more.

"Think I could get a job up there? Trabajo? Yo? Up at the mission."

The sisters nod up and down.

I'm pretty sure they don't have a clue what I'm saying.

We keep driving; everything is getting brown and ugly so we must be getting close to Texas.

"I think I might just stay up at that mission a while," I tell Mary Anne. "I could help out. I'd drive them around wherever they wanted to go, take them back and forth to Chihuahua for stuff. Probably they could use somebody with a little practical know-how. Nothing but nuns and Indians up there. I mean, they know what *they* know. You could probably learn a lot of secret-of-life type stuff from *them*."

Mary Anne says all she knows is that she wants to get over the border and be home. That's all in the world she knows.

Even though we are getting close, Mary Anne can't stop being scared that something will go wrong. I don't blame her really. Stuff does tend to go wrong a lot.

"You'll be fine," I tell her. "I'll get you up to El Paso just fine. Don't worry."

Mary Anne nods but she keeps holding onto the door handle for dear life.

"You'll be on the phone to your folks by tonight. They won't even be mad I bet."

Mary Anne nods again and I see she's trying to buck up. She's not a bad kid.

"Are you going to call your dad when we get back?" she asks me.

"I can't call him," I tell her for some reason. Maybe because we are just about finished here. "He died. A while back."

Mary Anne says she is really, really sorry. She says what if something had happened to *her* parents while she was down here. What if they were sick and she didn't know? What if *her* parents died and she wasn't even there. She would never forgive herself as long as she lived.

"Were you there when your dad died?" she asks.

"No," I say. "I wasn't. As it turned out."

"Where was he? Did you know?"

"Look, if I'd known I'd have gone there, wouldn't I?"

"It must be terrible to die alone," Mary Anne says. "I thought I was going to die down there. I couldn't see and I couldn't talk. They wouldn't even know where to send my body."

By seven P.M. we hit the border. The customs guys come out and look through everybody's papers. They have us get out while they look all over the truck. I explain about the nuns and the mission in the mountains. They let Mary Anne and me get back in the truck, but then two lady customs guards take the nuns away. Mary Anne and I sit in the cab and wait. Mary Anne is stiff and scared. But soon the nuns come back out and climb in the back of the truck. I don't know if the guards frisked them or what. I don't know if you even *can* frisk a nun. Maybe they just pick them up and shake to see if anything falls out.

Now the guards wave us on and in a minute we are back in the good old U.S. of A. Mary Anne says she wants to call her parents right now; she doesn't want to wait until she has glasses. She wants to make sure they are OK and to tell them the truth about everything. She wants to beg them to forgive her. Maybe they will be so glad to hear from her that they'll get in the car and drive down from Denver tonight. Maybe they'll be here by tomorrow.

I try to get her to go to the convent first. We could ask to use the phone there. But Mary Anne pleads to stop at the first phone booth I see. I figure she's been a pretty good sport, and anyway we need gas so I stop at a service station and tell the guy to fill it up. Then I walk Mary Anne to the phone booth on the far side of the lot. I get the operator for her and then step out while she makes her collect call. Mary Anne apparently gets somebody because she's talking and laughing and crying in there.

I stand waiting for her and thinking about the mission. I think about how it must be at night, high up under a million stars, the faintest scent of juniper in the cool air.

Over at the gas pumps, I notice, under the bank of white lights, there seems to be a commotion. The gas station guys are gathered around the little Datsun; one of them has a flashlight and they are all trying to see into the gas tank. Somebody comes running up with a long stick and they all stand back. The guy with the stick starts poking down inside the tank. In the office I see a guy yelling on the phone, craning to watch as he talks.

In the phone booth, Mary Anne is still yakking away.

At the pumps, a yell goes up. Looks like they've fished something up out of the gas tank. Meanwhile I see two big black birds flying, no, two little nuns, running, each in a different direction.

Mary Anne, I figure, will be OK. Her parents will come and get her. And nobody's going to think a blind girl was driving a truck.

Nothing to do now but step off into the steamy night. Cut through some back yards. Then walk along close to the bushes where the streetlights don't shine. Not that there are so many lights. It's a crummy neighborhood, little old sagging houses, half of them empty it looks like.

I need to look for a car I guess. But all of a sudden—maybe I'm tired— I just don't feel like stealing one.

I walk along looking at the sad little houses. Houses scare me. You never know who's trapped inside.

I am cutting through a little alley, passing by a house that has a porch with one of those cross-hatched lattice things to block the view. It's kind of hidden away back here and the house looks empty so I go sneaking up the steps. There's an old porch swing over there in a dark corner, and when I try sitting on it, it doesn't cave in or tip over.

I'm scared to lie down because it could collapse at any minute and it stinks so bad of mildew I'm afraid I might get a rash. But I do lean my head back and I guess I fall asleep. I must be asleep because I'm still driving—driving and driving along an old potholed road.

When I wake up, it's morning and on the other side of the porch is a lady sitting in a wheelchair. She's hooked up to a big green, bomb-shaped oxygen tank and has a shotgun across her lap.

"Don't step toward me 'cause I got nothing to lose," this old lady says in a loud raggedy whisper. "They give me two weeks, maybe a month, but I'm not counting on nothing."

She is little and old and her face is caved in; I guess she isn't bothering to put in her teeth any more. She's staring at me with sharp black eyes; they don't quite go with that landslide of a face.

"A month to what," I say. "You don't mean live?"

"Yeah live," the lady croaks out. "I can't hardly swallow or breathe even. Emphysema. And besides they say I got a mass. That's why they let me go. They saw that mass and they just threw in the towel. Sent me home hooked to this thing and now here I am."

"You're here all alone?"

"What's it look like."

She shifts the shotgun on her lap so it's pointing more or less in my direction.

"Watch it," she says. "'Cause I always wanted to shoot somebody. Not that I'm mean. I never *was* mean. But I get tired of everybody *else* being mean."

"Yeah," I say. "I know."

"You don't know *nothing*," this old lady says in her jaggedy old whisper. "You're another one of them. I know your type."

"Oh, now look," I say.

"No I won't look," the lady says. "Don't tell me to look!"

I give up trying to hold a conversation. I look around to see if there might be some way to just tip backward off the porch and then roll into the bushes and creep off. But there's this big lattice screen up all around. I can see, squinting through the crosshatches, that she's got an old beater out there, parked beside the house. I must of walked right past it last night. No telling when it was started last.

"Well," I say. "What do you want to do? We just going to sit here? Why don't you let me give you a hand? Want me to fix you something to eat? Want to go anywhere? I'll drive you. Your car run?"

"Yeah it runs. Why don't you try stepping toward it and see what happens."

"OK, I see you don't feel like being reasonable. So if there's nothing I can do for you, I guess I'll just be going."

"You want to talk about reasonable? I got bottle of bourbon and a couple of horse tranquilizers I can mash up and take when the time comes. So I don't need any advice about *reasonable.*"

She is staring at me with her little black old eyes. I don't know if she can lift that shotgun or not. She does have her finger on the trigger; I can see that.

"Well then. I guess I'll just go on along," I say.

"Not till I say so. My fine girl."

She's in such a huff to tell me off that the plastic tube falls out of her nose and she has to let go of the gun to stuff it back in.

"You know," I say. "It really isn't right of you to call me names. All I did was crawl up on the porch of a house I thought was deserted to get a little sleep. I know I'm not probably dying like you, which I'm very sorry for by the way. But I have my troubles. I was heading to a mission up in the mountains out of Chihuahua this guy told me about. Said it's so cool there, even now. Air like perfume. I was thinking I could get job up there. I was thinking of trying to go straight, matter of fact. Now, that all fell through. I know it's not as bad for me as it is for you, but I still feel bad. So why do you have to be so nasty? I didn't do anything to you."

"Figured you for crook."

"Yeah? Well, it takes one to know one. I believe I heard that somewhere."

Rotten old lady. Sure everybody's mean but her.

We sit there a while. I close my eyes and try to sleep a little. But it's getting hot and the air is thick and wet; this swing stinks something terrible. On the other side of the porch I can hear the old lady's lungs rattling.

It seems like we're going to sit on this porch in this thick, hot air until we both drown.

I seem to doze off and have some dreams, all to do with driving. None of them are about getting anywhere; just drive and drive and keep driving.

When I wake up again the old lady has rolled up to me so close I can smell her scary old smell. She's watching me when I open my eyes. The shotgun's still laying on her lap but she's not holding on to it any more.

"Listen," she whispers at me. "No reason for us to sit here in this heat and bicker. Let's get in my car and drive up into the mountains. Let's drive up to that mission. Get up where a person can breathe. I got some portable oxygen packs I can take. When we get there, I probably won't even need oxygen. It's the bad air here. That's my problem. You talking about the air makes me realize. No wonder I can't breathe this stuff. Probably this air is all that's wrong with me."

"Thought you said I was a no-good. I can't imagine why you'd want to take a trip with me. Frankly."

"Oh now," the old lady says. "I didn't mean it. You're nice company. You're the best company I've had in ages. I'm just mad about everything. It's nothing to do with you."

She studies me some more.

"In fact I think you must be an angel come along."

"Well. I wouldn't go that far."

"Let's drive on up there," the lady says. "Tell you what. I don't need a car any more. Go out and get the registration paper from the jockey box and I'll sign it over to you right now. I got money for gas too. Let's go. We'll drive up to the mountains. Up to where it's so perfumey."

"Somebody only *told* me that. I don't know firsthand. I don't know if there even *is* a mission."

"Oh it's there."

"How do you know? It might not be. The guy who told me was a crook."

"I read about it in the paper."

"Really?"

"Yeah. Read about it."

"When?"

"Oh. Some time ago. I'm not sure quite when."

"A Catholic mission? Mountains out beyond Chihuahua? Where they help the Indians?"

"Yep. That's the one."

I pack up her stuff. She doesn't want to take much. Just her pills and her oxygen and her bottle of bourbon. Her shotgun. A few nightgowns. A couple of dresses and a pair of high heels in case she starts feeling better. A sweater for those lovely cool nights. The wheelchair in case we might want to go strolling.

Then she has me open the icebox and get her money out from where she has it in a baggie flattened out underneath the ice-cube trays.

"Cold hard cash," the lady says and starts huffing and puffing which I guess is a laugh.

Seems like her mood has improved.

It's about three hundred dollars and she tells me to hold on to it to buy gas. Also we want to be ready if they ask us to contribute something at the mission.

I hold the money in my hand and she watches me.

"Yes," she says. "I do believe you came to me as an angel."

I load her in the car. It doesn't have much for brakes and one of the doors in back won't open. But it starts up after a few tries and the tires all seem to be holding air. The windows roll down and the radio works. It's set to a country station and the old lady says crank it up loud so she can hear. It's Johnny Cash playing and it turns out we both are crazy about Johnny Cash. She says twenty-some years ago she got to go up on stage and dance with him at one of his shows.

Unlikely.

We make a U-turn in the little alley and I don't hear anything fall off the car. We pull out onto the road, radio blasting, and head for the border.

In the Garden

I'm out whacking blackberry bushes with the machete when Lulu and Guy come driving up with a jar of Red Zinger and a bottle of gin. Palmer is in his shop sawing away on something so Lulu goes and pounds on his window. He must have looked up because she starts a little war dance, waving the gin over her head. Lulu is a big goofy redhead in cat-eye glasses and you never know what she'll do next. She acts all flirty toward Palmer but I don't think it's personal. I think that's just how she is.

Guy comes over to me and asks how it's going down in the garden. He gave up on his own garden, so now he always makes a point of sympathizing with me about mine. I complain to him that with all the rain—it seems like it's been raining more than usual—the blackberry vines grow over the path in just one day. By the second day they've linked up so you can't get through. You've got to be out there whacking every minute.

Of course we talk about the slugs because that's the main thing that drives everybody crazy out here. They overrun your garden every night, and in the morning you find dozens of them, sprawled out on the lettuce leaves like they've been on a drunk.

Guy wants to know what's my latest strategy against the slugs. When he still had his garden, he was a big slug fighter. He was always picking up local lore on how to get rid of them. Once he tried making a little mountain range of coarse salt all around the garden. The salt was supposed to suck the fluids out of the slugs when they tried to crawl through. The slugs were supposed to dry up and die. You would come out the next morning and there would be nothing left but a hundred little slug crusts.

Supposedly. Instead, what Guy found were a dozen tiny pathways cut through the salt; the slugs had just plowed on through. And now his garden was sewn with salt.

We'd both tried the well-known method of putting little saucers of beer all around the garden. The slugs would try to drink the beer; then they'd fall in and drown. That was the idea. But that didn't work either. Maybe you did get a few slugs floating around in the beer, but there would still be plenty in the garden eating lettuce.

"I think the beer just invites them," Guy said. "They come from all over when they hear there's free booze."

"What about eggshells?" Guy asks me. Somebody once told him that a border of crushed eggshells would keep slugs out.

I tell him I've got a border of crushed *glass.* I tell him the whole story of how Palmer brought home some old window glass from a house he was demolishing and how I put three or four panes in a sack and pounded the glass into shards.

I show Guy how I ran a six-inch-wide border of canvas around the whole garden. Then I got gloves and sprinkled on the glass so there'd be a thick ridge all around. I tell him I worked two whole days on that project.

"Looks good," Guy says. "Does it work?"

"Nope. A lot of them are dead in the glass but the others just climbed over them and headed on into the garden."

"You've got to hand it to them," Guy says. "They have the courage of their convictions."

By now Lulu has gotten Palmer out of his shop and we all go sit on the porch. I get glasses and ice and we all sit down to have a drink. After all the rain, we are glad to have a warm, sunny day. That's probably what made Lulu and Guy start thinking about drinks. We do have to be a little careful about our drinking out here, especially in the winter, but on a day like this it's probably OK.

Lulu and Guy live about a mile down the road on a bluff overlooking Puget Sound. They live in an old church that they bought with the idea of fixing it up into a cool place to live. Guy has shown us where he wants to put a big window in the roof so there would be great light, even when the sky is, like it usually is, overcast.

They got a start on the renovation, but it turned out to be a bigger job than they'd thought. They discovered that the hillside under one corner of the church was eroding, and they had to put in a new foundation on that side. After that, they ran out of money and haven't been able to do anything on the church for quite a while. Lulu has a part-time waitress job at the Gull's Nest and Guy can get a little work as a draftsman for the town, but they still don't have enough money to gut the church and fix it like they want.

At the same time, they don't want to start putting up makeshift stuff that they'll have to take down. For now, they're just camping there in the empty church like a couple of refugees.

Well, it *is* hard to get much money out here on the island. To get any real money you'd have to get a job in Seattle. I was thinking of trying to get a job of some sort, but it's hard from out here. You either have to take your car on the ferry which costs a lot and takes forever to load and unload. Or you have to go on foot and wait for a West Seattle bus which doesn't come very often. And then, if you're going into Seattle, working a job and then spending four hours a day commuting, you think: what's the point of even being *on* the island?

Lulu wants to pour everybody gin, but I hold on to my own glass and pour my own gin, because Lulu always pours too heavy. Lulu likes everybody to get drunk. But I don't necessarily want to get drunk just because Lulu shows up with gin.

Guy asks Palmer how it's going at the marina where Palmer is doing some carpentry work and Palmer says it's going OK. He's repairing a dock, and its work he likes because it's out on the water. He likes watching the seagulls. He thinks it's cool how they drop clams onto the rocks to break the shells open; then they dive on the meat that's inside. How many humans, Palmer wonders—say they were stuck somewhere and starving—would figure out that method of opening clams.

This is one thing I love about Palmer. He is always noticing little things and making you think: *Would* you be as smart as a seagull?

Palmer doesn't ask Guy what's going on with the church because we know he's feeling kind of depressed about it. Lulu never seems to care about anything, but Guy seems to be feeling pretty stuck.

We are a little stuck ourselves at the moment, but it doesn't show as much. We have our little old house that we love. The floors slant and blackberry vines have pushed through where the walls meet, but we like it that way. We would never want to live in a bourgeois type of house. We wouldn't want a house that a banker or a lawyer or some executive would live in.

We have our big garden, of course, for food, and Palmer gets his carpentry jobs. Lately we've been thinking, too, about getting some goats and learning to make our own cheese. We could eat it and sell what was left. I guess it's an OK way to make some money though I'm not too excited about the idea of milking goats. Still, lots of people are getting them. Goats are the latest thing, it seems.

We all drink our drinks and say they hit the spot. It's sure great to see the sun for a change, we all say.

Then Lulu starts talking about different people we know. She asks us if we've heard about Jonathan and Posy. They are splitting up she has heard. In fact, she heard that Jonathan has a new woman and that he's already moved her into the house that Jonathan and Posy only recently finished fixing up. We all went over there for a housewarming not long ago and they'd done a really nice job on it. They turned this falling-down old place into a beautiful house with lots of tall windows and a nice cedar deck. And now this other woman has already moved in.

"Where's Posy?" I ask. "Is she still on the island or what?"

Lulu says she doesn't know. She heard that Posy was talking about taking Jonathan to court over the house, even though they weren't married and even though the land and the house technically belong to Jonathan.

Maybe she didn't have the rights of a wife, Posy is supposed to have told somebody, but she ought to have some rights since she was out there every day working on that house as much as him if not more.

Most people would have to agree with that. Posy is a big tough girl from out on the Peninsula and you always saw her up on that house in a carpenter's belt. I used to drive by and see her up there in the rain when Jonathan was nowhere around.

"Jonathan's a jerk," I say.

"Oh, boo-hoo," Lulu says. "If he wants to get rid of her, let him get rid of her. It's not charity. He was smart not to get married. I don't know why *I* got married."

Lulu always says things like this, so nobody takes it seriously. It is, though, a little odd that she and Guy are married since Lulu is always going on about what a hippie freak she used to be and how she's never going to go bourgeois, no matter what other people do. Whereas Palmer and I have never really thought about getting married, even though I'm sure anybody seeing us takes us for Ma and Pa Kettle.

"Why didn't he get rid of her before she built that whole house, or most of it," I say. "If he wanted to get rid of her so bad."

"I guess he wanted a house," Lulu says. "Do you think?"

"If I were her," I say, "I'd go burn it down."

"Sure and go to jail," Lulu tells me. "Don't think you're going to get away with burning something down. People think they're being slick, but the cops will know exactly what you did. These arson experts can read what you did like a book."

"Sounds like you've looked into it," Guy says.

"Bet your sweet ass," Lulu says.

This is the kind of talk she loves.

Palmer laughs; Lulu almost always makes Palmer laugh, even though he never talks like that himself and would hate it if I did, I know. He's a big, Viking-looking guy but he's actually very sensitive. He was a violinist when I met him in college. The first time I saw him, he was playing in a concert, his eyes closed, his long wavy hair flowing down, his long, beautiful fingers living a life of their own. It was unusual in a big man and I fell for him right then.

Now he takes out his pouch of Drum and uses his beautiful fingers to roll a cigarette. He gives it to Lulu and then rolls one for himself. Guy and I don't smoke.

Lulu lights up her cigarette and says, "Oh, let's not talk about people, for god's sake, like a bunch of old biddies. Let's *do* something."

We're getting old, she says. We are sitting out here on this dumb island and getting old. Well, that's not why *she* came here, just to sit and molder.

Guy asked her why she came then, and she says to have orgies, obviously, so that we all get a laugh.

We are, I guess, getting a little old. We're all about thirty; maybe Guy is even a few years older. We are all products of the late '60s. Lulu and Guy did the whole Haight-Ashbury thing and I can just see Lulu there in granny glasses, her hair in a big red Afro.

Palmer and I never went that direction. Our plan had been to go to Canada to get out of the draft; we thought maybe we could get jobs as teachers in Saskatchewan or some other place no one wanted to go. But once Palmer's brother, Mel, was killed in Vietnam, Palmer got a deferment. So then we didn't have to go to Canada or try to become teachers and we just took off in our VW bus. We went everywhere, down to Central America, up to Alaska. We camped and lived cheap and picked up jobs when we needed to. We were free and that was all that mattered. Anyhow that's how it seemed then. That's how it seemed to me.

Now we've landed here on this island in Puget Sound. Like a lot of other people we're here with our gardens and our goats and our funky old houses. I'm not sure quite why, but this is where a lot of us have ended up.

"Let's have some fun for a change," Lulu says. "Let's tell about our favorite movie."

She tops off her drink with gin. Guy reaches out and gets the bottle from her and tops off his drink too. She gives him one of her stares, takes the bottle back and tops hers off even more. Guy laughs and shakes his head; he doesn't top his off again and Lulu wins that one.

Watching them is kind of like watching a gunfight at the O.K. Corral except that you always know who's going to win. I wonder, sometimes, if that's even why she's with him, because he'll always play but she'll always win.

Lulu makes Palmer laugh, but he never wants to play these games that she thinks up and now he changes the subject to somebody we all know, a guy named Bruce. We all went to a party he had few nights ago even though nobody likes him very much. People think he's kind of weird. He doesn't have a girlfriend, though he tries hard enough, and he lives alone in a big old ramshackle house that he hasn't done anything with. We only know him really because he throws these big parties with ribs and burgers and lots of booze, and people go but he has never really fit in here. I'm not sure why.

Anyway we were at his party, and Bruce at one point turned down the stereo and said he wanted to tell us something. People kept talking and laughing and nobody could hear so he stood up on a chair and said he wanted to tell us about something that had happened that was really cool. Finally everybody quieted down and Bruce said he'd written a screenplay and guess what, it had gotten optioned. He said he was going to LA next week to meet with his agent. It was something he'd been working on a long time, he said, a story about his grandfather's experiences in the Depression.

This was so in from left field that nobody knew what to do and everybody just stood there. Finally a couple of people clapped and then Bruce got down from his chair and turned the stereo back up.

"Fucking Bruce," Palmer says now. "Fucking Bruce up on his high horse."

I look at Palmer because he seldom curses. I wonder if he has chugged his gin too fast.

"Yeah," Lulu says. "He's full of shit. Why's *he* standing on a chair. *I'll* stand on the chair next time. We'll all stand on chairs."

"His *agent,*" Palmer says. "Right."

"You don't think he has an agent?" I ask.

"He probably does," Guy says. "If his screenplay really got optioned."

"Yeah," Palmer says. "*If.*"

"Well, there's no reason he would say so if he didn't," I say. "Nobody cares."

"That's right," Palmer says. "Nobody cares."

"Palmer!" I say. I can't think what's going on with him.

"Come *on,*" Lulu says. "Let's play movies."

"Sure," Guy says. "Let's play movies."

The bottle comes around; I notice that we're forgetting to pass the Red Zinger along with it. I notice that, but I still pour more gin in my glass when it comes around and don't bother with the Red Zinger myself. I'm getting to the point where I'm glad Lulu showed up with her bottle and her crazy talk. I'm tired of that damned garden for one thing.

Lulu says she'll start. Whenever we play, she always has to go first; that's understood.

She says the movie she picks is *Swept Away.*

There's a movie theater on the island and we all go when a new movie is there. So we have all seem the same ones. We all saw *Swept Away* not too long ago.

"What's in it for you?" Guy asks. This is the question someone is supposed to ask when we play movies.

Lulu says her favorite thing is how the woman and the guy who are marooned on the island just fuck their brains out and how he dominates her even though she's this rich bitch who orders everybody around and he's only a servant. Lulu says that must be the best sex in the world and she wishes somebody would capture her and dominate her. Not forever, just for a while, like in the movie. Then you could helicopter out of there like the woman in the movie did.

"At least we're on an island," Guy says. "You've got that part."

Palmer is getting red in the face. I don't know how much of it's the gin and how much is the way Lulu is talking. Lulu is always like this; still, you are never sure quite where things will go.

Guy says OK, it's his turn.

Lulu holds out her hand to Palmer to show she wants another cigarette. He opens his pouch of Drum and starts rolling one for her.

"Guy's movie is going to be about something tragic," Lulu said. "Some girl dying of tuberculosis. Watch and see."

"Don't be silly," Guy says. "It's about a girl dying of *hal*itosis."

We all get a laugh at this and everybody takes a drink. We're having a lot of fun.

"OK, OK," Guy says. He says, surprise, his movie isn't about dying anybody. It's an old movie, *Streetcar Named Desire.*

"Stell*a!*" Lulu starts to yell. "Stell*a!*"

"What's in it for you?" I ask.

"I just like the name," Guy says.

"De*sire!*" Lulu yells. "On a streetcar. I like it too."

"No," I say. "I don't think it means having sex on a streetcar. It's about going through life like you're *on* a streetcar. And the streetcar is your desire for things. Lots of things, maybe. I don't think it's even about sex."

"No?" Lulu asks. "Then what's Marlon Brando doing in there in that T-shirt? Jesus, Mary, and holy Joseph!"

Guy says I have to give my movie now and I say an old one too, *The Searchers.*

"Good!" Lulu says. "Captured by Indians."

"No, that's not why," I say.

"What's in it for you?" Guy asks.

"That they look for the girls the Indians took and never give up. That's all they can think about. I know they are confused, partly, but they never stop looking."

"Quaint," Lulu says. "Too bad they don't have a streetcar, they could get there faster."

"OK," Guy says. "Let's get this over with. Palmer?"

Palmer says some World War II movie he saw as a kid; we've probably all seen it but none of us can really remember it. Even Palmer can't remember the name.

"What's in it for you?" I ask.

Palmer says he liked the part about the soldier who got separated from his platoon and who survived alone in the winter woods with just a knife and an overcoat. He built himself a shelter with pine boughs and figured out how to trap birds and roast them on a stick.

"That was boring," Lulu says. "OK, game over. Now let's have a rant-fest. I'm first. Can you believe the people down the road from us came to the door and wanted us to buy tickets for some PTA thing? Christ, I never thought I'd end up someplace where they actually had the nerve to come around and sell stuff for the PTA."

"The people that bought the blue house have a baby," I say. "It seems like there are lots of kids around all of a sudden."

"Was that a rant?" Lulu asks.

"No."

"Good," Lulu says. "Because it wasn't much of one."

Lulu says she doesn't really expect any good ranting from me and I'm out, so now it's Palmer's turn.

"Fucking Bruce," Palmer says.

Palmer is drunk. It's strange because usually when he's drunk he gets quiet, not loud.

"Him and his bullshit," Palmer says. "Bragging about some b.s. of a supposed movie."

"We don't know that it's b.s.," I say. "It could be good. The Depression is interesting."

"It's b.s.," Palmer says. "A guy like him writing a movie. How far do you think he's going to get? Give me a break."

"I don't know how you know it's b.s.," I say. I must be drunk too because I hardly ever argue with him.

"Maybe it's good," I say. "Maybe it's as good as that movie about the guy lost in the woods you love so much. That guy who was so happy wandering around by himself killing birds."

Palmer looks at me like I have gone crazy but at the moment I don't care. Anyway, he seems to have gone crazy himself.

"I don't see why we can't be happy for him," I say. "It doesn't hurt us, does it? *We* don't have to go to LA. *We* don't have to have an agent. *We* don't have to let somebody make a movie that we wrote. We can just sit out here in the bushes fighting slugs. Even though the slugs are winning by the way. Even though the slugs know what they're doing a hell of a lot more than we do."

"*Rant!*" Lulu yells."

"It's not like he was stuck-up about it," I say. "He was just happy. He told us because he thought we would be happy for him."

"*Happ-*eee!" Lulu yells out. "We're *happ-*eee!"

"We're just jealous," Guy says.

"I'm not jealous of that jerk," Palmer says. "Speak for yourself, buddy."

"Speak for yourself, buddy!" Lulu yells. She kind of falls off her chair and Guy grabs her. She puts her head down on his leg. He smoothes her wild red hair and picks up her silly glasses.

"I want to go home, Guybaby," she whimpers. "Right now."

Guy gets her on her feet and tells us goodbye and half carries her off to the pickup. They're pretty drunk but they only have to drive down the road to their place so they are probably OK. There aren't many other cars. That's one good thing about living here on the island; it's fairly safe to drive around drunk.

Palmer and I keep sitting on the porch after they leave. The bottle of

gin, I notice, is just about empty. I put it down on the floor where we can't
see it.

Palmer, I also notice has started to cry. He does cry sometimes when he
drinks and starts to think about his brother, Mel. It's complicated because
it's not just that Mel died. It's also that Mel, by dying, saved Palmer from
the draft, and left Palmer free to do whatever he wanted. It's kind of like
Mel died *for* Palmer.

The only thing Palmer knew to do back for Mel was to stop playing
the violin. I never understood exactly how that worked, but that's what
Palmer did. Wouldn't Mel have *wanted* you to play, I used to ask. But I
haven't asked that for a long time. This is the decision he has made. Sometimes I almost think Palmer decided not to do *anything* just because of
Mel. I never used to think this, but now I am starting to.

We sit together on the porch. I can feel myself starting to sober up. It
feels terrible.

We sit until dark and then keep sitting. Every now and then Palmer
rolls another cigarette. He can do it in the dark, just by feel.

I should go make something for us to eat so we can get kind of back on
track, but I can't seem to get up and go in the house.

"Palmer," I say. "What are we going to do? We're going crazy out here
a little."

I can hear him blowing out smoke.

"How about we load up the bus and just go," I say. "Take off. Like
we used to. Remember how we used to feel. Just driving. Never knowing
what we would find by night. 'Each day is its own lifetime,' you used to
say. Remember that? We were happy then. Happier."

The tip of his cigarette glows red for a second.

"Sounds good," he says.

But of course we both know we can't go back to doing that again. I
don't know why. We just can't.

"Maybe we should join the Peace Corps," I say. "We could go help people in Africa or somewhere."

"Maybe."

"Maybe we should have a baby," I say. "*That* would be something.
Think how we would love it. We would love it so much we would die for
it, without batting an eye."

He laughs and I do too. Obviously it's a dumb idea to have a baby just
so you could die for it.

At the moment I don't have any more thoughts for what we could do.

"You know what I hate?" I finally say.

"What?"

"I hate all that glass down in the garden. It doesn't stop the slugs. It just mangles them up. Some die but the rest keep coming. They still eat up all the lettuce. Glass or no glass."

"Kamikaze slugs," Palmer says and we both laugh a little.

"Why don't we go right now and try to get that glass up?" I ask him. "I don't know what I could have been thinking to put a bunch of broken glass in a garden."

Palmer says OK. He feels his way off the porch and over to his shop. He goes in and gets his big flashlight. He gets a canvas sack and a pair of heavy gloves and we go down the path to the garden. I hold the flashlight and Palmer puts on the gloves. He starts scooping up the shards of glass and dumping them in the sack. After a while I put on the gloves and scoop up glass while he holds the light. We're both kind of drunk so we aren't too efficient but we do get a lot of the glass scooped up.

Ticket

Them asleep, Pen would go out to the woodshed for an armful of logs. Then she'd get the idea to detour down to the cellar. Hit the light and stand still a second until the mice stopped skittering. Then—well, well— there was that bottle of Jameson lying on its side, hidden behind some ten-year-old jars of pickled beets.

She'd head back up and put the logs on the fire. Open the stove door so she could see the flames lick. Turn out the lights. Call the dogs. Sit back.

Twenty minutes, half an hour, and she'd just be laughing. Wondering what the hell the problem was anyway. Always forgetting she was going to wake up at two or three in the morning, slumped over in the cold, the bottle down five inches, the fire out; even the dogs gone off.

It was to head off those trips to the cellar that Pen would, instead, slip out the back. She'd climb into the pickup, leaving the door ajar so as not to slam it and wake up her mother, Verna. Verna with her loaded hunting rifles propped up in her bedroom closet; Verna always hoping somebody would finally come along who'd heard it was three women alone on an isolated farm.

Pen wouldn't turn the key yet. She'd just release the hand brake. Then go gliding down the lane like a ghost in the dark. Only when she'd passed the mailbox and rolled onto the blacktop would she slam the door shut, turn the key, hit the headlights.

None of this was really needed, the way Verna and Grandma slept.

The way everybody slept. There probably wasn't a soul awake in the whole valley so late to see her go by.

She'd drive on through town. She never went there in the daytime anymore. Couldn't take it, the way everybody glanced up, then looked away when she walked in the store.

Everybody was sorry of course. Most people were on her side probably; probably lots of them thought it was a shame. That didn't keep them from giving her the little sideways look, checking to see if she were going to go kill herself or kill somebody else or what.

But it was night now, and everybody was in bed. And soon she was through town and then up and out of the valley and onto the blacktop road blasted into the side of the high rock canyon wall. Not too forgiving of a road. Sheer rock face on one side; drop-off into Powder River on the other.

Then some nights she'd have it both ways. First finding the Jameson, then going out to get in the pickup.

Drunk, she drove up the canyon with the lights off, all the windows open to the white ice night. Felt the smooth, hard steering wheel slipping through her palms. Just like a caress, she thought. Just like it.

Then when a too-close-to-the edge shimmy jarred her awake, she'd tell herself to cut it out. Then she'd take a deep breath, hit the lights, do a U-turn on the narrow road, and drive on home at a reasonable speed. Creep in real quiet, sleep a few hours until Verna's six A.M. market report came on in the next room.

Coming in, though, from one of those little moonlight drives on a January night, the phone was ringing.

She couldn't think what it could be. She'd never known that phone to ring past ten P.M.

Things had happened of course. The time Dad died of a heart attack out in the milking parlor. The time Verna dropped a plow on her leg and almost bled to death one spring afternoon.

Things happened, sure. It was just that they usually got wrapped up at a reasonable hour; people still got to bed by nine-thirty or ten at the latest.

But the phone did seem to be ringing. She checked her watch. Two-twelve, what looked like two-twelve. Could have been twelve-two. Anyhow, it was late.

At one point, say six months ago, you might have thought, well, maybe it's Bill. Now though, as was well-known by everybody in the valley, Bill was lying in bed with his new schoolteacher wife by his side. He'd be curled around her, no doubt, like he always slept, the back of his big foot curved against the bottom of hers. That's where he was, no more than three miles away. One and a half miles if you were to fly—like a lone black bird—straight and low over the dark winter fields.

No, it wouldn't be Bill calling.

And now she was wondering. Had that even *been* the phone?

But the next night—this was a just give-up-and-drink night—damned if the phone didn't ring again. This time there was no question because the dogs jumped up and started to dance. Pen waded through them and made a grab for the receiver.

"I am calling for Kitty," some woman said.

Pen—already loaded of course—had to reel back into time.

"I am calling for Kitty," this person said again.

"Well, you missed her," Pen finally figured out to say. "Kitty hasn't been here for almost twenty-five years. We don't know if she's even alive or what, so I'm afraid I couldn't help you there."

"No," the person said. "I've got her here. I'm calling *for* her. She's sick and can't barely talk. Not loud enough for the phone anyhow."

"Well, you probably want my mom, Verna Thomas, but she's . . . ."

"No, I'm trying to reach somebody named Pen Clouston. Kitty wants Pen to come. She's real sick here all alone. Is this Pen Clouston I am speaking to?"

"Yeah. That's me. Come where?"

Right then, though, the little table the phone sat on got knocked over. The phone fell off. Dogs got mixed up in it. Pen finally got hold of the receiver again but by then nobody was there.

Some type of prank maybe. Kind of elaborate.

Now that Pen had moved back home, Verna gave her the job of feeding the cattle twice a day. For help she had Charlie, one of these old cowboy types who'd worked for them since before Dad died. He wasn't good for much anymore except to gab but you couldn't cut him loose now.

"Damn shame," was all Charlie ever said about it. The whole Bill thing.

Charlie of course had known them both since they were kids.

"Yeah. Well," Pen said. "Guess you never know."

"No. I guess not," Charlie had agreed.

Then that was that.

Winter mornings, Pen and Charlie were out early to feed in the frost-bristled fields. It was nice in the early morning, the mountains high and blue; the close-in foothills skiffed with white; the sagebrush poking through like purple-gray knots on the backside of embroidery.

They had the first batch of big old dimwitted Herefords fed by around ten and would come in for coffee. Usually it was just the two of them sitting at the kitchen table, since Grandma drove into town most mornings on some business, to pick up groceries or see about things at the church. Verna was always out tinkering with her trucks in her big heated shed. She had her KWEI from Weiser with its fiddle music and market reports. Later in the day she'd listen to Paul Harvey and spend a half hour getting worked up about Creeping Socialism.

When Grandma wasn't there, Pen would turn on the oven and she and Charlie would sit with their chairs tipped back, their boots propped up on the oven door to dry, their mugs of coffee warming their hands.

"Somebody called up last night," Pen mentioned. "Real late last night. She said she was calling for my aunt."

"Who's that? Kitty?"

"Yeah. You knew Kitty?"

"Oh sure. I knew Kitty."

"We haven't heard from her for years. Since I was a little kid."

"That right?"

"Yeah. I never really know why. You know?"

"No, I wouldn't know anything about that."

"They never talk about her."

"Oh?" Charlie said. "I wouldn't know."

They watched steam rise from their boots.

"What does your mom say?" Charlie asked.

"I didn't tell her yet."

Pen got up and refilled the coffee.

"Who was it that called?" Charlie finally said.

"I didn't find out. The connection went bad."

That night, after Grandma and Verna were in bed, Pen sat down and popped a beer. She waited but naturally the phone didn't ring.

After she'd sat for an hour nursing that one beer, she decided they'd had their chance. She got up and went down to look around the cellar.

Two days later, though, Marla Williams called and said Pen had to come down to the post office and sign for a special-delivery letter.

"What's this?" Marla said from inside her post office cage, still holding on to the envelope. "New York City? What on earth? Something you sent for?"

Pen got it away from her finally and drove home; she sat in the truck to open the envelope addressed in flowing handwriting. She knew—suddenly remembering weekly letters that used to arrive a long time ago— that the writing wasn't Kitty's.

Inside there was no letter. Only what appeared to be a plane ticket, round-trip Boise–New York. There was nothing else but a slip of paper with an address and a phone number.

"Look what I got," Pen told Charlie the next morning. "Somebody sent me a plane ticket to New York. It must be that woman calling for Kitty."

Charlie held his cigarette in his teeth and took the envelope, held it out at arm's length in his big red hands. He and Verna both needed glasses; neither one would admit it though.

Charlie took the greenish ticket and studied it, his head tilted away from the smoke.

"Expensive ticket," he said. "Seven hundred dollars."

"Oh yeah? It gives the price."

"Yep."

Pen took it and saw where it gave the price.

"Lot of money," Charlie said.

"What do you think?" Pen asked. "Do you think it's safe there? You hear about all these drug dealers and things. From what you see on TV."

"Probably all hype," Charlie said.

"What? About the drug dealers? You never watched that show. What was it called? Cars chasing through the streets; shoot-outs."

"No, I don't look at television."

"Well, that show was about New York City."

"Probably hype."

"Maybe they overdo it, but I guess it's based on something."

"Not necessarily. Could be all hype."

"You don't know that. Have you ever been there?"

"No, I never was there but I met some boys from New York City one time in the service. *They* was all hype."

"So you'd go, then, if you had the chance? If somebody sent you a ticket?"

"No, I wouldn't go."

"But if you say there's nothing to worry about, wouldn't it be fun to see the sights? Empire State Building? Statue of Liberty?"

"Probably a disappointment."

"Why? The Statue of Liberty?"

"Well. I tell you. One time I went to Reno."

"I'm not talking about Reno."

"It's the same idea. You hear about a place. Like Reno."

Pen got up to clear the coffee things away but she knew she was still going to hear about Reno. About the time some guy told Charlie that behind the bottles in a certain bar, instead of a mirror there was a big fish tank, and that they had girls in there, holding their breath and swimming underwater.

Pen had heard this story before. She couldn't remember how it ended though.

"Wellsir," Charlie said, "I finally I decided to go see what it was all about. I got up before daylight and drove to Reno; got there by nightfall. I had the name of this place—Patty's, I think was the name of it—that was supposed to have this big fish tank with the girls in it. It wasn't naked or nothing. Just bathing suits. Two-piece bathing suits I guess it was supposed to be."

"OK."

"Well, when I got to Reno I asked a fella at a gas station if he'd heard of a place called Patty's. He said he had and he told me where to find it."

"Yeah?"

"Well, I found it, and went in. Set for a while. Drank a beer and watched those fools put their money in the slot machines. Some of them running two, three machines at once. Men. Women. Old ladies in hair curlers, all their money in a coffee can. Course that's why they want to get you there. That's why they spread these stories. So I watched that for half an hour. Then I just got in my truck and came back home. Didn't spend more than six bits the whole time I was there."

"No fish tank?"

"Nope. All hype."

"Well. That's Reno. I doubt if the Statue of Liberty is all hype."

"Probably not what you expect. Probably a disappointment once you take all the trouble to go there. Half this stuff, they show it real big in the picture. You get there, it's like four feet tall. Nothing like what they showed."

"I don't think the Statue of Liberty is four feet tall."

"Well. I wouldn't know."

"The thing is, it sounds like Aunt Kitty's real sick."

"Oh, well, if she's sick you've got to go. What'd your mom say?"

"I didn't tell her yet."

"Well," Charlie said. "I wouldn't know anything about Kitty."

When they'd done feeding and finished their mid-day dinner, Pen made some excuse and drove the forty miles to Bonner. She went in to the county library and looked up a book on New York City. She saw a picture of the Statue of Liberty that looked quite a bit taller than four feet.

There were lots of pictures of people walking around seeing the sights, taking pictures, having a good time. Not a word about drug dealers or be careful or anything.

The three of them sat together for breakfast though they each had something different. Verna had her big plate of ham, potatoes, and eggs along with three cups of black coffee. Grandma had toast and homemade blackberry jam and a pot of tea. Pen irritated them both by eating Frosted Flakes.

"Somebody from Aunt Kitty called up," Pen said once they'd all started to eat.

Grandma and Verna both looked up and out the window toward the misty blue mountains far away. Both seemed to look at the same spot.

"What do you mean somebody," Verna said finally, going back to sawing on her ham with a steak knife.

"Kitty's too sick to talk on the phone," Pen said. "So some lady called up for her. Kitty wants me to come to where she is in New York and help her and she sent a plane ticket. Seven-hundred-dollar plane ticket."

Grandma sat still, her teacup lifted three inches from the saucer.

"Figures," Verna said. She took one last bite of ham, put on her hat, and went out.

Pen remembered seeing Grandma cry. It had been a long time ago when Pen was little. It seemed like Grandma cried a lot in those days. She sat in her blue chair and cried into a handkerchief. Pen used to marvel at the change in those handkerchiefs, how one would come out of the drawer snowy white and ironed into four crisp squares, bright with pink embroidered roses and trailing leaves. Then, next time you looked, it'd be crumpled into a gray, tear-filled wad that seemed like it could never recover.

But that was a long time ago. Pen couldn't remember Grandma crying since then. Now, though, Grandma cried. After breakfast, instead of putting on her girdle and stockings for her trip to town, Grandma went instead to sit in the old blue armchair. She sat with her hand pressed to her heart, looking out over the high foothills they called Sheep Mountain. In the barnyard you could see Verna's legs in jeans and boots sticking out from under her pickup, her roll of sockets laid out on the ground beside her.

"I think I should go, don't you?" Pen said.

Grandma took off her glasses and sopped up the tears with her handkerchief.

"Grandma, what? Are you worried about Kitty?"

Grandma clamped her lips shut as tears rained down.

"What? Are you worried about me?"

Grandma seemed to be thinking and finally nodded that she was.

"Well, I'll be careful. Don't worry."

Grandma sobbed once out loud.

"What? I'm not going for more than a week. At most."

Grandma nodded as if trying to see that it wasn't so bad but not really able to.

"Shouldn't I go help Kitty? If she's real sick and alone there?"

But Grandma only cried more and wouldn't talk.

"I guess I ought to go," Pen said to Verna. "Since Kitty's so sick. And all alone, it sounds like. I don't know who this woman is. A nurse or something maybe."

Pen and Verna were standing out in the barnyard. Verna had taken off her hat and the wind whipped up her hair. Years of lifting and pitching had given her the wide shoulders and the biceps of a twenty-five-year-old farmhand. Now, though, the short dark hair was threaded with silver. In the afternoon sunlight, you saw the fine lines crisscrossing her face and you could believe she was pushing sixty.

"Fine trick," Verna said.

"What's a trick? To be sick? Maybe dying?"

Verna scraped mud off her boot heel.

"She's probably no more dying than anybody else. She's three years younger than I am. Anyhow. She's been dead a long time already as far as I'm concerned."

"Why?"

"Why? Because she went off and she wanted it like that is why. She went chasing off and broke Mom's heart. You see her crying? This is bringing it all back."

"Bringing all what back?"

Verna looked up to the dark hayloft window where some old chunk of equipment dangled from an ancient rope, clanking a little like it always had in the late afternoon when the wind came down from the mountains.

"I don't know why I don't get up there and take that thing off," Verna said. "It's going to crash down and kill somebody one of these days."

"How did Kitty break Grandma's heart?"

"How? By taking off, like I said."

"You don't have any idea why?"

Verna smoothed her wind-whipped hair, fingered her hat. These were signs that their talk was almost over.

"Nope."

"You must have some idea."

"I guess that's just how she wanted it."

"Well. I'm only going for a week or so. Because she's sick and I guess she needs help."

"Kind of late for her to remember she has a family."

"Yeah. But if she's real sick."

"Think she'd know if we were dying? If Mom was dying, say?"

"No, I guess not."

"I wouldn't guess so either."

"Two wrongs don't make a right, they say."

"I don't want you going. It's not safe in these cities. Maybe you don't hear the news."

"I'll just stay at Kitty's and help take care of her. Besides. It wouldn't hurt me to go somewhere for a little while. I'm not doing so great here. Maybe you've noticed."

Verna turned to look into the sun.

"I can see you're dying to go. Kitty's playing you like a fiddle."

"That's silly. I wouldn't know Kitty from the man in the moon."

"You want to go. I can see that."

"You begrudge me going somewhere for a little while on a free trip? See some sights? Take a tour to the Statue of Liberty maybe? When I'm walking around here like a ghost? Everybody sorry for me. It's gotten so nobody even wants to look at me when I go to town. Did you know that?"

"That'll pass. You're still young. You've still got time. Get married again. You'll have your kids, have a family."

"Got a man for me? I haven't noticed too many around."

Verna studied inside her hat. Ran her finger along the sweat-stained leather band.

"I saw Bud Exley in town."

"Come on, Verna."

"He's working for the Company Ranch now. He's a hard worker. Always has been."

"How else is he going to finance a green Chevy Impala with a little green knob on the steering wheel?"

"He's a good strong boy. He knows how to work."

"He's slow in the head. That's why he's not married yet."

"Well. The stutter keeps him from getting his thoughts out."

"You know he's slow as well as I do. The only smart thing he's ever done was stutter so people could say, oh, he isn't slow, he just stutters."

Verna put her hat back on.

"Then go find somebody else. Meanwhile you've still got the place that'll come to you some day. Still got your work. You still walk out and every morning and see the mountains. Breathe the air. You're still who you are. These other things . . . ."

Verna squinted into the sun.

"I tell you one thing," she said. "Going off to New York to hobnob with Kitty and her crowd sure isn't going to help."

"She must not have a crowd or she wouldn't need me."

"I doubt very much if she's back there all alone. Knowing her."

"Well," Pen said. "I'm going. Tomorrow. I called and set it up. Charlie can get his nephew to help feed."

"Suit yourself," Verna said.

She reached up, squashed her hat down onto the crown of her head. About finished.

But then she took off her hat again and held it out to the high misty mountains.

"For god's sake, look," she said. "Where do you think you're going to find something like this again? What do you think you'll get in some city?

Some little job for wages where they can wad you up and throw you away like a Kleenex? What do you think you're going to find that's better than this? That's yours? Here you are who you are. These cities—you're nothing and nobody. Think you'll find a man there? What kind of men do you think they have there. They'll chew you up and spit you out."

"Well. I've been spit out already. Right here at home."

"You're still yourself. You know who people are and they know who you are."

"Oh yeah. Everybody knows who I am all right. They know all about me. Every little thing."

Verna put her hat back on.

"I'm only going for a week or so," Pen said, but Verna was already walking away.

After supper Grandma sat in her blue chair with one of her embroidered handkerchiefs in her hand; she looked out toward the mountains even though the windows were black.

Verna was working on her accounts at her desk in jeans and sock feet.

"What are you using for cash?" Verna said. "Because I sure as heck am not throwing good money into any such scheme."

"I have money. I went in this afternoon and took some out of the bank."

"You're driving over to Boise? Where are you leaving your truck?"

"I thought I'd park it at that parts place over on Overland. Get that kid B.J. to drive me to the airport."

"Like to see how much of it'll be left when you get back," Verna said.

Verna opened her desk drawer, rummaged around, then pulled out her pistol.

For a second, it looked like maybe Verna was going to shoot her rather than let her go off to get stolen away by Kitty. But instead Verna took hold of the barrel and handed the gun over. Handed over a little cardboard box of bullets too.

"Might as well take it," she said. "You never know."

Then she got up and walked off to bed.

The plane took off at 9 A.M. which meant getting up at three in the morning to drive the four hours to Boise, leaving time to drop off the truck and get driven to the airport.

It was nice walking out the back door at three instead of coming in. Sober. Stone sober, now, she promised herself. She'd have to have her wits about her now.

The sky that was usually kind of blurry was full of ten thousand cold, white stars. Each of them all alone and not a one of them giving a damn about who she was or what had happened.

Pen loaded the suitcase into the truck, then felt her way into the pitch-black barn, all the way to the back. She felt around for a rotting old barrel that was against the back wall and dropped Verna's gun and bullets down inside.

She stood for a minute in the dark, breathing in the freezing air. It was crisp with odor, so that she seemed to breathe in the hundred years of spilled feed and dried manure, mouse droppings and pigeon wings, bag balm and axle grease.

Finally she went back out and got in the truck. She released the brake and eased silently down the lane.

Let them sleep.

When she was down on the blacktop, she turned the key, hit the lights, and cranked up the radio. Instead of turning left toward town, she turned right, heading up the canyon. Forty miles later, she turned onto the ramp for I-84 East, heading to Boise.

The kid from the parts place drove her up to the airport and dropped her in front with her suitcase. Inside it was bright and bustling with travelers; one of them told Pen where to find the check-in desk. Pen gave the girl there her ticket and when the girl saw the name she said there was a message. The message was that they'd gotten a call at home not long after Pen had left. The call was to say that her aunt had died. She was being cremated this morning and there would be no service. Her aunt's assistant was packing up her things and shipping them home. Her aunt didn't need Pen's help now.

The girl at the desk said she was really sorry.

"Thanks," Pen said.

The girl asked if Pen would want a refund of the ticket. That could be arranged, the girl said, in a situation like this. It would need to be done right away, though, so they could put the seat up as a standby. The flight, she said, was booked.

"I don't know," Pen said. "Just a minute."

"Certainly," the girl said. "I'm terribly sorry. Were you close?"

Pen looked up sharply. But this girl, of course, didn't know Pen or her family or anything that had happened to them. She didn't know that Bill had gotten scooped by a schoolteacher or that Kitty had broken her mother's heart. She didn't know and didn't care. She was just a girl behind a counter trying to be nice.

Pen took her ticket and walked over to the huge plate-glass windows. The sunlight was pouring in and you could look out over the snow-covered foothills and the mountains beyond. They looked a lot like the mountains of home, heaven-like in the pure morning light.

Out there too were the airliners, glittering like immense silver bullets.

The girl at the desk was watching, worried.

"It's OK," she went over and told the girl. "No refund."

Letters

1.

Just when it seemed like we might have to marry poor Chuck, Viv got a love letter from a man she'd never met. It came to her at the Portland Hotel where she operated the cigar stand on the evening shift.

"This is a new wrinkle," Viv said when she got home that night.

Her long walk from the hotel was miserably cold; a wet wind whipped off the river and right up her skirt, and her feet in open-toe high heels were two chunks of ice. So she didn't mind seeing me waiting up with cocoa, even though it was nearly midnight and I should be asleep.

Still in one of her shiny, cinch-waist dresses, she plopped on the couch and reached up under her skirt to undo the garters. She pulled off her stockings to massage her long delicate feet that always hurt. Luckily she had a stool in her cigar stand. Luckily she was still good-looking enough to get a job where you weren't on your feet all night.

"What's his name," I asked.

"Mr. Magoo," Viv said.

I saw the letter had put her in a good mood.

"Does he say what he looks like?"

"Three feet tall with a four foot beard."

"What's his job?"

"Ax murderer."

"Let me read it."

But Viv said no, it wasn't nice to read other people's letters. She went into her room and tossed me the blankets and pillow for the couch where I slept.

Because she never shut the door to her room, I usually knew what she was up to. On this night, I saw her hide the letter where she usually hid things, in her big jewelry box that she could lock with a little gold key. Then she hid the key under the round blue canister of talcum powder.

The next afternoon when she was at work I got the letter out.

His name was Paul, he wrote, and he had stood watching her at the cigar stand when he'd been in Portland on business. He felt like he knew her from somewhere and as he watched he tried to remember; then he realized what it was. She looked exactly like Lauren Bacall in that movie—he couldn't remember the name—where the classy girl stands by her guy, even though he's down on his luck. Then the guy gets a face job and turns out to be Humphrey Bogart.

"Say," he wrote. "If I got a face job and turned into Humphrey Bogart, would you go out with me?"

Viv and I were happy enough as we were, or so it seemed to me, just the two of us in our little basement apartment. Our place was small—one bedroom, a living room where you could sit on the couch and watch feet walk by, a tiny kitchen. Viv liked it that way. Everything was handy, she said. And you didn't have that much to clean. The kitchen was just enough for people who didn't want to be cooking all the time. We didn't have to cook much because Viv got her meals at the restaurant, and most nights she snuck something home for me, good stuff, like half a steak somebody had left, or a big piece of cake, the frosting thick on the napkin it was wrapped in.

When Viv was in a good mood she would get out her little record player and moon around to Glenn Miller. Sometimes we danced, Viv holding me lightly, dipping and swaying, her eyes closed, pretending I was somebody else.

It seemed fine to me. Still I knew that Viv needed to get married pretty soon; it was just something people had to do.

Viv had been married, of course, to my dad but it didn't work out and he decided to try Alaska.

"He wasn't such a bad guy," Viv thought to tell me once in awhile. "It was just one of those crazy wartime things. You married people you didn't even know. Everybody did."

Another time she told me: "He was lots of fun when he wasn't drinking. He was a good dancer."

Now and then I could see Viv reminding herself to open up a drawer in her mind labeled Cam's Mother and rummage around for the right thing to do or say.

"He drew the funniest doodles," she told me another time. "In his letters. He was stationed in San Francisco and didn't seem to have anything to do but write letters. Most of what I knew of him was letters. All the girls where I was working loved his doodles."

This was during World War II when Viv had come to Portland from the farm in Eastern Oregon where she grew up. A notice had been sent around recruiting women to do war work in the shipyards on the coast, and it was just enough to make Viv's mother let her get on the bus to Portland. Right away she got a job at the Kaiser shipyard and it was the greatest job ever. She started out as a cleaner, but somebody saw her and said she'd be great to hostess the brass when they took the brand new warships down the Columbia to test them out. So Viv was put in charge of making up the menus and hostessing the lunches for all the big shots as they sailed down the river.

The officers flirted with her and asked her out all the time. One time, she told me, she added up that she got asked out twenty-seven times in one shift.

But Viv was a country girl never in a city before, and she was being careful. Besides, her high-school boyfriend was somewhere in Europe. Instead of going out on dates, she went back to her dorm and wrote him every night as she had promised she would when he left. She wrote that she would wait for him forever. That's what you were supposed to do during the war and that's what Viv had done.

"When I think of what I passed up," Viv said. "Then I ended up marrying some sailor."

"Not," she reminded herself to say, "that your dad was a bad guy, really."

"What happened to the boy from high school."

"He was killed," Viv said. "Blown up by a land mine. There wasn't anything to send home."

"Were you sad?"

Viv said she guessed she had been. She said it had barely seemed real that there was nothing left of somebody who was just your age. Somebody you had kissed.

Anyway, after that she started going out and met my dad.

•

So now Viv needed to get married again and that's where poor Chuck came in. He was nice enough and OK-looking, pudgy but not really fat. He had a steady job at the post office. The good thing about him was that he was anxious to get married. That made him different from most of the men Viv met at the hotel.

The bad thing about him was that he was boring.

At home we kidded about him all the time, laughing how finicky he was about every little thing, how extremely clean he was, and how he liked to pamper himself with lots of aftershave and hair cream.

"The man smells just like a dime store," Viv said.

That was how we talked at home. But when Viv was with him she was twinkling and merry and seemed to like him a lot. He was crazy about her; that was clear. He gave her long, doting smiles like he was just about to pour cream on her and eat her up.

He was a good decent man, I think, if not the brightest. This is something to remember about Viv. She was trying.

Chuck had a two-toned blue Buick and money saved up; besides being clean he was thrifty. When Viv said the word, they would get married and buy a house, any house Viv wanted, within reason.

In the meantime Chuck spent some of his money taking us out to eat every Sunday. He took us wherever we wanted, which was almost always a drive-in out on Stark where they attached a tray to your car window and piped in the latest hits. Chuck would have preferred a booth in a nice, clean luncheonette, but Viv and I loved the drive-in. Viv liked singing along to the hits and looking around at the people in the other cars; I liked lying in the back with my hamburger on my chest and my feet out the window.

Chuck was a pretty good sport about it. He didn't look back at my feet very often, and he never mentioned more than once that if you had a table, you wouldn't have to worry about dripping ketchup on yourself.

I always thought we'd had a pretty good time on those dates, but sometimes, when we got back home, Viv would lie down on her bed and cry.

I sat on the floor outside her door listening; when the crying tapered off I took in the Kleenex box. She sniffed and blew her nose, lit a cigarette, blew out a whole lot of smoke, and said I was a pal.

"I'll tell you something," she said one of these times. "Even though I shouldn't."

I sat still as a mouse; I loved it when she told me things she shouldn't.

The thing I hated the most was when she went into a mood and stopped talking.

"I have never been in love," she said. "I'm sorry but I didn't really love your dad. And he didn't really love me. This was right after the war when you were *supposed* to be in love. Everybody seemed like they were and you felt like you should be too. But that didn't mean you really were."

I nodded. I was afraid if I said a word she'd remember she shouldn't be telling me this.

"If I marry Chuck," she said, "I never *will* be in love. In my whole life."

But of course we both knew she had to get married and time was running out; she was over thirty, though she said she was twenty-eight.

"Maybe I missed my chance for love," Viv said. "Maybe if you don't fall in love at the right time, it's too late. You just miss the boat."

I said I didn't think she had missed the boat. I said I was sure she hadn't at all.

Viv reached out and patted me; I was a pal, she said.

I waited a week before I asked: "Did you write that guy back?"

"None of your beeswax," Viv said.

She hadn't, apparently, because a few days later I found another letter from Paul in the jewelry box; in it he said he was almost glad she hadn't written right away because it showed she was innocent and good, the type of girl you rarely found these days. He said of course he had noticed she wasn't wearing a wedding ring or he would never have written. Maybe he shouldn't have anyway. It was just that watching her, he could tell that she was sad, and he was just betting someone had broken her heart.

"Maybe it takes one to know one," he wrote.

I was surprised he knew Viv was sad. Since she was so beautiful and gay in public, I thought nobody knew but me.

The next letter came to the apartment. It was lying on the floor under the mail slot when I got home from school. I carefully steamed it open, something I was good at since I had to steam open letters that came from Viv's sister, Shirley. Shirley still lived out on the Eastern Oregon farm, and she didn't think much of our life in Portland. She thought it wasn't healthy for me, never getting exercise and so on. So I always had to make sure that Viv wasn't getting talked into sending me to live at Shirley's for my own good.

From Paul's letter, I saw that Viv had written him and asked what had broken *his* heart. Paul replied by telling her the story of Junie, who sent him a Dear John letter during the war. He was in Italy when he got the letter.

Up until then he'd been OK. He'd been in almost four years by then, and he'd seen a lot of combat. But he had learned to compartmentalize his mind: one half heard the screaming and crying, felt the fear, the exhaustion, the wet and the cold; the other half was planning his and Junie's wedding. In his mind, he designed the dress she would wear—it was a little simple, maybe, but gracefully sweet. He had selected the flowers she would carry: pure, simple daisies.

After he finished planning their wedding for the thousandth time, he started planning their little house, the bright varnished wood kitchen suite, the royal blue sectional sofa for the living room, splurging, maybe, on a glass coffee table. The blonde bedroom set. The matching spread and curtains, cream-colored and sprinkled all over with tiny wildflowers in rainbow colors.

Every chance he got, he wrote to Junie with all of his plans, telling her how much he loved her and how good their lives would be when the war was finally over.

Oh yes, he'd bought the whole line about the loyal sweetheart at home, waiting for her boyfriend to come back no matter how hard things were, no matter how long it took. You saw it in every movie and you believed it. *He* believed. And he held on to that belief for dear life. *That's* what he was fighting for.

So when he got the letter from Junie—she had decided to marry some fat-bottomed guy at the bank where she worked—he had what the Army called a "mental and physical breakdown."

"In other words," he wrote, "a nut case. I don't tell most people this. But somehow—don't ask me why—I feel that I can tell you. Somehow I feel we are two of a kind."

It had taken him a long time to get over Junie. Even though the war was over and most of his buddies had settled down—getting married and starting families like you were supposed to do—he couldn't seem to get with the program. Couldn't seem to find the right girl. Couldn't seem to believe again though he'd tried several times.

But there was something about Viv. He sure as heck would like to find out what it was.

When I had read the letter a couple of times—apparently she hadn't mentioned me—I glued it back up with mucilage and put it with the other mail on her dresser.

Viv didn't say anything and neither did I. But she was thinking about him, I could tell.

When the next letter came, I saw she had written him that Shirley wanted her to come home and marry a rancher who had recently been widowed.

This was news to me and scary if it was true. Paul wrote back that of course Viv had to do what was right for her, but *personally* he was having a hard time seeing her out there sloppin' hogs.

"Sounds like you and your sister are pretty different," he wrote.

Viv must have said something about liking to dance because Paul wrote: "Hey, what a coincidence! I love to dance too! And I've even been known to make it all the way through a number without crushing the girl's feet! Well, I couldn't see you out sloppin' hogs, but I *can* see you on the dance floor. Let me look; oh yes, there you are. You're wearing something shiny, kind of dark green, I think, to set off that white skin and goldy-red hair. It's cinched tight around that little waist, then a big swishy skirt; taffeta, maybe? Then: Hey what do you know? There I am too; the tall dark guy with the beautiful redhead in his arms and the dreamy—Hey, did I finally die and is this heaven?—look in his eyes."

Then the letter got kind of sexy; I took a deep breath: "Hoooooo boy, do you think my luck is going to hold? Sure can't wait to hear from you again. Now let's see, it's about midnight, and by now you're probably home from work (Yes, I made a note that you closed down your stand at 10!) and now you're probably getting ready for bed. Another coincidence! So am I! Now—let's see. How am I going to get you ready for bed. Hmmm: peaches-and-cream complexion, goldy red hair, long movie star legs. I guess I'll put you in a nice pair of sky blue silk pajamas (save the shorty negligees for some other type of girl!) And then . . . Uh-oh. Here's the MPs. Slow down, Bud! Let's stop it right there!"

By the next letter she had sent him a picture: "One million thanks," he wrote, "for the dear, dear picture. Though—I don't need it to remember you by. I remember you just fine! But I love *having* something, if you know what I mean, something you gave me. Scares me though. Damn (Excuse my Italian), what a good looking girl you are!

"And here's the picture you asked for. I put on my best black suit and my best silk tie and got it taken just for you. (Say, you'll hurt my feelings if you send it to Shirley for target practice!)

"Oh so you *think* you remember me, maybe. Now that *is* flattering! A guy doesn't often make such an impression!

"Just kidding, doll. I'm *glad* you can't remember me because it shows what a sweet good girl you are. Some girls are too good for us men and you're one of them."

I shook the letter and the little picture fell out; he was pretty good-looking—quite a bit better than Chuck.

In the next letter I could see she'd told him about me finally; she gave me, apparently, as the reason she was thinking about marrying Chuck.

"Sure he wants to marry you and adopt your little girl," Paul wrote back. "I am sure she is adorable if she is anything like her mother. But Chuck is not the only one! I have never wanted anything else in my life but to make a home for a beautiful wife and family! I know you know this about me."

I was starting to like Paul a lot. I liked hearing I was adorable and was sure I could be, given half a chance.

"I want you to know," Paul wrote, "that when I got to the part about Chuck, I was a good soldier. I lit a cigarette, sat back and read right along. I said to myself: if dependable old Chuck is good for my girl, if she wants to settle down in a little house with him and bring his slippers and pipe every night when he gets home from the P.O., then I will wish her all the best. I'll hope she has the happiest little life there ever was. I'll bow gracefully out with one last Sayonara.

"But oh baby—do you know that when you told me how, when good, old Chuck was looking into your eyes trying to think of something romantic to say, that you sometimes drifted off to thoughts of me—do you know that I jumped up and opened the hotel window, stuck my head out in the rain and *screamed*! So that people walking down below looked up and I bet they were thinking, That guy's either crazy or in love or *both*!"

He had to see her, he wrote. He couldn't wait any longer. He was driving down from Seattle next Sunday.

"If I bomb, then fine; you can give good old Chuck the green light. But maybe I won't and just maybe the sky will be the limit. I'm comin'! Pick you up at eight."

Oh yes, and he'd be driving a red Studebaker convertible; he hoped she didn't mind a Stude. He was manager of a Studebaker dealership in West Seattle so had to be true to the cause.

Poor Chuck, I thought.

These days Viv was spending a lot of time sitting at the big mirrored dressing table that our landlady, Mrs. Stack, let us use. I watched her as she carefully, carefully drew on the tawny eyebrows. Then I watched her wipe them off with cold cream and draw them on again. I watched her fuss over her fingernails, buffing and blowing, polishing on coat after coat of bright, bright red. I noticed she had a new dress, dark shiny green, shot through with glittering gold thread. She didn't wear it to work but left it on a hanger on her closet door. It hung there like another, perfect Viv, the wide patent-leather belt cinched at the waist.

That Sunday, Viv told Chuck she was sick. By now I officially knew that Paul was coming. We spent the day scrubbing our little basement apartment spotless. It was nice, a whole day of Viv and me home working together and listening to dreamy Glenn Miller, Viv with her hair tied up in a rag and her face bare.

Then, Lord, what nervous wrecks we were, starting around four and getting worse every minute as it got closer to eight.

Viv sat smoking at her dressing table, looking at herself in the mirror. She sat in her slip and stockings and high heels; she would wait for the last minute to put on the green dress so it wouldn't crush.

I was supposed to answer the door when he knocked. Until then I wasn't supposed to look out the window in case he might see and think we appeared eager. When he came I would make conversation for a few minutes and say Viv wasn't quite ready.

When the knock came, I counted to ten, then went to the door.

There stood Paul.

He was, I thought, even better-looking than his picture, tall and dark. His shirt was gleaming white against his dark skin. Only his slightly bulging eyes made him look not quite like a movie star.

He stepped inside. When I said Viv wasn't quite ready, he nodded and asked if he could sit down. I said sure and offered him candy from the bowl on the coffee table but he said no thanks.

He sat down on the couch and I sat down too. It seemed like neither of us could think of anything to say. He didn't even ask me how old I was or what was my favorite subject at school.

"Sorry," he said after a minute. "I'm scared stiff."

"Yeah," I said. "So are we."

In the weeks that followed, letters started coming from Shirley. From them I saw that Viv was already thinking of marrying Paul, and that Shirley was having a fit. Viv hadn't known Paul at all long enough, Shirley said, and she certainly couldn't afford to make another hasty mistake.

But who cared what Shirley thought? She was only a hick farmer. She didn't know how magically Paul had changed our lives.

During the rest of January and into February, Paul drove down from Seattle every Saturday, left his suitcase at a motel, and came to take Viv out, usually to the Embers where they danced to a little combo.

Poor Chuck wasn't in the picture anymore.

Of course I couldn't go on such fancy dates and was supposed to be asleep when Viv got home late. But I would get to see Paul when he came back at noon to have breakfast with us. While Viv was in the kitchen scrambling eggs in her fanny-hugging tan slacks and a new yellow-rose apron, Paul would sit on the couch with me in his white-white shirt-sleeves, a coffee cup in his hand. He liked looking at magazines and always brought over a stack so that when we were sitting around he could leaf through them. Sometimes he would show me a house like the one we would get, or a picture of a family having a barbecue in their back yard.

That's what we would be like, he said. Once he and Viv were married.

The house would be in a good neighborhood and we would quickly fit in as one of the good, nice families. I would have the prettiest girl's room in the world where I would want to invite all my friends.

"What do you think of that?" he said.

"Great," I said, even though I didn't have any friends. With a single mom and living in a basement apartment, I was too different from most kids. I didn't care because being Viv's pal was enough. Still, I liked the idea of girls from school being jealous of my fancy room and my dad's convertible.

Once he was on his feet in his new job, Paul told me, Viv could stop working. She'd be busy throwing dinner parties and barbecues for all the nice friends in our neighborhood and going to parties at *their* houses.

"We're going to join the human race," Paul told me. "About time, don't you think?"

I said sure.

•

Of course Shirley, Uncle Roy, and my cousin Mike had to come trooping over from Eastern Oregon for the wedding. I was mortified that Paul had to see them: Shirley with her short hair sticking out here and there, hobbling in high heels so she looked like a lumberjack dressed for Halloween; Roy grinning and nodding in the baggy, bluey suit *he'd* gotten married in back before the war. Then Mike, his face a mess of pimples, dressed up in a too-small white shirt that wouldn't stay tucked in, a clip-on tie, and a windbreaker.

Whereas me, I had a new rose-colored velveteen dress, black patent-leather shoes, and a wrist corsage of miniature carnations.

Viv was a surprise. She looked pretty of course, but in a different way from when she got ready for work in her dark, glittering dresses. Now in a lacy, peachy dress with a crown of white blossoms in her hair, she seemed smaller and softer, younger, her face wide open in a way that was new.

So, I thought, you're finally in love.

Nobody told me that I would be going home with Shirley right after the wedding and staying there until the honeymoon was over. Viv had packed my suitcase when I wasn't looking and I only found out at the reception when someone passed the word to go stand on the sidewalk in front of the restaurant. In a minute we saw Paul pull up in the red convertible with the top down; Viv stepped out the door to throw the bouquet to her girlfriends from the hotel. Somebody opened the car door and she stepped in. Then they were gone, trailing the tin cans that Paul, I knew, had tied on himself; I'd seen them in a bag in the apartment.

And there I was in my rose-colored dress and flashing shoes, having to squeeze into the cab of Shirley's pickup with the three of them for the six-hour drive over the mountains.

Everyone tried their hardest to be nice to me but I wouldn't be nice back: I was just holding my breath until Shirley got word to drive me to Bonner and put me on the Greyhound back to Portland.

When I got back, Paul had already moved into our basement apartment and had to use the dresser drawers that were mine, so my stuff was in a box beside the couch. But it was only temporary; in every free moment we drove around looking for the perfect house. *All* the houses looked perfect to me, but Paul couldn't decide on anything. Every house had something wrong. There wasn't enough closet space or the living room faced north, meaning it would be gloomy in the winter. The bedrooms were too small or else they were too big. The bathroom was dark or the kitchen seemed like it would be too hard to cook in; you'd have to walk too far from the refrigerator to the stove. Sometimes the shape of the living room was strange and he just couldn't see sitting around there.

Paul got home from his job at the De Soto dealership about five and, with Viv already at work, seemed to think he should take care of me, even though I had been taking care of myself after school for a long time. He would pick me up and we would drive around looking for a house we might want. We drove slowly through the nice residential streets, because Paul said we had to consider not only the house itself but also the neighborhood. We looked for clues as to how nice and happy and hardworking the people living there were. If we saw a man washing a car in the middle of the day, it was bad because men should be working during the day. But if there were kids riding bikes or two women chatting on a porch, it was normal and good.

"We want a neighborhood where people know how to be happy," he said. "I'm sick of these people who don't know how to be happy."

Then, when we were tired of looking at houses, Paul would drive to a park on a hill that overlooked Portland. I would wander around in the park for a while and Paul would sit in the car, smoking and listening to music on the radio.

After a while he'd call me, and we'd drive more.

I'd be ready to go home but I didn't say anything. Even though I had kind of given up on Paul thinking I was adorable, I was still trying not to be a brat.

As the evening came on, Paul would start telling his war stories. He told me how he joined up with the Canadians even before Pearl Harbor and got shipped to England in time for the Blitz. The main thing he remembered was the smell. It smelled kind of like when his mother used to singe chickens out in the yard, he said.

Later on, he said, he was in Operation Husky and he asked me if I knew what that was.

I said I didn't and he said it was the invasion of Sicily and that I should learn more about World War II because it was the most important thing that ever happened.

"OK," I said.

In four years, he didn't think he was in the same place for more than a week. He was always on the move. No one day like the next. Sleeping in a top bunk. Sleeping in a hole. Sleeping in the mud.

"When you're there, all you think about is home. Then when you get home, all you think about is there. Funny huh."

I said yeah it was.

"Ha ha," Paul said.

When the war stories ran out, Paul would talk about Viv.

"As soon as I get established on my job, she's not going to be working nights any more, that's for sure. That hotel is no place for a girl like her."

"Yeah," I said, although I had always loved her little stand in the hotel lobby, bright with candy and cigars and magazines, people always stopping to talk and joke. I had thought it was the best job you could have. But of course I knew it wasn't what normal moms did.

"What kind of a man would I be if I didn't get her out of that?" Paul said.

Once he suddenly pulled over to the side of the street, yanked the hand brake, and turned to me. He seemed angry.

"Look," he said. "I love your mother. And I am going to give her a nice normal life. Understand?"

"Yeah."

"And I'll tell you something else. A family is the most important thing a man can have. A man is nothing, without that. He's not a man."

Then he lit a cigarette and smoked and I looked at myself in the side-view mirror until finally he finished his cigarette, smiled, and patted my head to show everything was OK. Then we stopped somewhere to get a piece of pie—pumpkin for Paul, cherry for me but only if I drank all my milk.

By spring Paul was working long hours, starting around noon and going until late into the evening, selling as many cars as he could to get promoted. Now there wasn't much time to go house hunting and nobody said anything about houses anymore.

In the summer we had fun sometimes when Paul and Viv both had the same day off. When the sun was out we drove around Portland with the top down and watched everybody look at us. Of course they were looking at the red convertible, but also at Paul and Viv, both in sunglasses, Viv with a gold scarf around her hair, her hand stretched out to rest on his shoulder. Sometimes he picked it up to kiss, his eyes still on the road.

Once we all went to a drive-in movie. The movie playing was something about Mexico and Paul especially wanted to see it. He was interested in Mexico because a buddy of his, a guy named Harry Luck, had gone down to there after the war. You could live for practically nothing, Harry had written, and the weather was always good. That was the life. That buddy of his *was* lucky, Paul said.

I had a pillow so I could lie down in back and I made little breathing sounds to see what they would talk about if they thought I was asleep. I was always on the lookout for anything about Shirley and a more healthy life for me, or, now, something about how crowded the apartment was with three of us there.

But they didn't talk about that. Instead, while they were waiting for the feature to start, Paul told Viv a bunch of war-story stuff about Harry Luck, how it was Harry who kept Paul from killing himself when he got the Dear John letter. How they had ended up in the same hospital in Italy, Paul cracking up and Harry with a shot-up leg. How Harry had made Paul get up out of bed and push him in his wheelchair. How Paul had pushed Harry around the little hospital garden about ten thousand times. And, how, when it was all over, Harry had convinced Paul he would fall in love again some day.

Then they just watched the movie about Mexico and smooched.

The happiest days of all were days when Paul got a letter from any of his Army buddies. Then he would sit on the couch, smoking cigarettes and drinking coffee, reading out parts of the letter to Viv and telling her about the guy who'd written it and the experiences they'd had together. Sometimes the letter had in it the letter from another buddy so there were two guys to tell about. When Paul was finished he was supposed to send those letters on to some other guy so that they all stayed in touch.

"Those guys," Paul told Viv, "were my family. They were all that got me through."

Sometimes we still went to that drive-in restaurant out on Stark even though Paul didn't like the hits they piped in. He was strictly a Swing man, he said. Of course, I wouldn't lie down with my feet out the window in a car like this. And besides, Paul didn't like too much silly stuff; he could be pretty crabby sometimes. Viv said it was because he was working too much. He was driving himself, she said, to make a good living for us. She didn't want him to feel that he had to kill himself for us, but that's how he wanted it to be.

Then one night in August, Paul wasn't there to pick Viv up from work and she finally walked home, even though Paul had said he didn't ever want her walking alone at that hour.

Viv's first thought was that he'd had car trouble coming home from Tigard. Her second thought was that he had been robbed for his fancy convertible.

Viv left me to listen for the phone while she went to stand on the sidewalk in front of the house, watching for two wide headlights to come flashing around the corner.

After a while Viv came back in. She said not to worry; Paul would be here when I woke up.

But when I went to get my pillow and quilt from the shelf in their room, I noticed Paul's cuff-link box was missing from their dresser.

I rushed to tell Viv.

"We've been robbed!" she cried, running in. "They robbed him and then came and robbed the apartment."

But other than Paul's cuff-link box, nothing was missing from the dresser. When Viv opened the jewelry box, everything, including the little diamond ring from my dad, was still there.

The closet, though, was empty of Paul's army of white-white shirts, and the dresser drawers were empty of his socks and shorts. When I got down to look under the bed, I saw his shoes weren't in the rack he'd set up there.

Down on my knees, I saw Viv's legs running from the apartment and I thought two things. One was that Paul had come back; the second was that the robbers were here to kill us.

Viv was out the door already, but she wasn't running away up the street. Instead she was running back behind the house to the garage where Mrs. Stack let us store a few things. Viv went in through the side door and I followed. She stood there in the dark garage, holding her lighter over her head. There in the flickering light was Mrs. Stack's old blue Plymouth that hadn't been driven for years. Against the wall was the too-small-from-the-beginning bike Chuck had bought me, and on a low shelf were some jars of pickled crab apples Shirley had brought from the farm. Above that, so high up under the shingles that you had to use a stepladder to get to it, was another shelf where the suitcases were stored. There were Viv's new white suitcases, purchased by Paul for the honeymoon. There was my striped suitcase inherited from Viv. Then there was the empty space in between them that had been filled by Paul's large brown bags, also purchased special for the honeymoon trip.

When I woke up on the couch the next morning, Viv was still in her work clothes, sitting at the kitchen table smoking cigarettes.

Any makeup she'd had on had worn off during the night. It was scary to see her dressed for work but with no eyebrows.

She took out a cigarette pack but it was empty.

"He's sick," she said. "Or hurt. I know he didn't just leave."

Viv told me to see if there was a loose cigarette in her handbag but I couldn't find one.

"What did Paul talk to you about?" she asked me. "When he picked you up after school."

"The war. What it smelled like getting bombed. Stuff like that."

Viv walked in her stocking feet to the coat closet. She opened the door and stood still for a second, because of course there was the empty space where Paul's jackets had been. Then she started going through the pockets of her coats, looking for cigarettes.

"What else did he talk about?" she said from the closet.

"He talked about houses. We drove around and looked at the people that would be good neighbors. He talked about you."

"What did he say about me?"

"How you looked when he first saw you, so pretty. How bad it was that you had to work at night and all. How you deserved a nice home."

Viv found a pack with three cigarettes in it and came back to the couch.

Shirley couldn't be allowed to find out, Viv told me. If Shirley found out, Viv would know it came from me and she'd never speak to me again.

"I wouldn't tell Shirley," I said, starting to cry for the first time.

Viv said she was sorry, she didn't know what she was saying anymore. She put her arms around me and for the first time *she* cried, crying and crying onto my neck while I patted her hair.

For the next few days, we both stayed home, sitting at either end of the couch, and waiting. Viv had called in sick and we just sat, willing Paul's red car to pull up in front of the house.

How would he look when he climbed out? Would he be bandaged up, his arm in a sling? Would he glance nervously toward our windows because he had something to tell us that we might not be able to take? Or, would he slam the car door angrily because one of us had done something wrong and that's why he left? Could it have been me, maybe, something I had said, or not known to say, when we were driving around?

Or would he get out of the car with a gentle smile on his face, knowing how bad we'd been feeling and also knowing that in a minute he could explain whatever complicated thing it was that had happened so that we would be happy again and drenched in relief?

A couple of weeks went by. Viv stayed home and I found out she had quit her job at the hotel; I went to school off and on. When one of the girls from Viv's job came by to see if we were OK, Viv stood in the doorway and talked to her through the screen.

"Paul's mother is very sick," Viv said. "He had to go back to Kansas to look after her. I don't know how long he'll be away."

The girl said she was awful sorry.

"Are you OK, kiddo? You look like you're having a rough time. Can I come in for a minute?"

"We were just leaving," Viv said. "I'm going over home for a while. To visit my sister."

Of course, that was just to get rid of the girl; Shirley's was the last place she would go.

That same day there was a letter from nosey old Shirley giving the usual stupid farm news and saying how she hadn't heard from us for a while. Was everything OK?

It seemed to be the letter from Shirley that got Viv up and out. Later that afternoon, she got dressed in an old skirt and blouse and low-heeled shoes and walked twenty blocks into the seedy side of town to a place called The Torch Café. There she got a waitress job she'd seen advertised on the 7 P.M. to 3 A.M. shift.

"It's OK," Viv said. "It's something. At least I won't see anybody I know. Maybe I can pay the busboy to drive me home."

Viv said we had to pull ourselves together. I had to go to school every day now because that's what Paul would want.

Meanwhile she would work and not fall behind with the bills and we would keep ourselves in good spirits. We would believe in Paul and wait for him and remember that however bad things were for us, they were probably much worse for him.

"There are bad men who hit their wives and run around," Viv told me. "And there are men who aren't really bad but just don't do what they should do, like your dad. But Paul wasn't either of those. He wanted his life with us more than anything. You saw that, didn't you?"

And yes, I had to agree that I had.

"Could it be," I asked once, "that, like, he had a wreck or something and he—?"

"Died? No. In the first hours that's what I was afraid of. But they would have found him by now if he'd had a wreck. And anyway, I would know if he were dead. I know he's not."

"What about amnesia," I said. "Like in that movie we saw where the guy didn't know who he was."

Viv said yes, she thought it was something like that. Something related to his wartime experiences. He had been through so much, she said. Terrible things. Some things he hadn't wanted to tell even her.

Fall came and we waited and had faith and were not so terribly unhappy. Viv cried sometimes, but she had always cried now and then. Afterward, when I had taken in the Kleenex box, we would sit on the bed and talk about Paul. Viv never doubted that he was hurt somewhere. We imagined him lying in a white hospital bed with a bandage on his head. Maybe he would take out the wedding photo that he carried in his wallet; maybe he studied it, trying to remember how to get back to us.

At Thanksgiving, Viv wrote Shirley with a complicated story about how Paul had gotten promoted at the dealership and how the bigwigs had to be around on holidays to make sure nothing went wrong. She was very sorry, but of course we couldn't leave Paul.

Then we had to get through Thanksgiving on our own—something we had never done. Before Paul came, we'd always gotten on the bus and gone to Shirley's on holidays.

"Let's go to a movie to distract ourselves," Viv said. "Just be careful because only creeps will be there on Thanksgiving."

Because it *was* Thanksgiving we splurged on popcorn and cokes and sat pressed together, making sure no one came near us. It was a movie about romance of some sort and Viv cried all though it. Still, we kind of had a good time.

Shirley, judging from her next letter, had the idea it was Paul who didn't want to come out to the farm. She hoped Viv hadn't gotten too good for her own relatives, she wrote, even if they were plain people.

Well, we *are* too good for them, I thought. Or, would be. If Paul were here.

Then Christmas came. Viv wrote Shirley the same story and we went to the movies again. It was a Jerry Lewis movie and we laughed and laughed.

Remembering Thanksgiving, I realized Viv seemed different now, almost happy.

"Has something happened?" I asked her.

Viv said no, she just had a good feeling. She felt sure we would hear from Paul very soon.

Then, a few days into the new year, something *did* happen. Something bad. But I didn't know what.

Usually when I got home from school, she was sitting on the couch in her robe and slippers, smoking and drinking coffee. She would be listening to records and doing her nails. Around five, she would get dressed in any old thing; at Milo's she had to wear an ugly pink smock so it didn't matter what she had on underneath. Then she would put on her raincoat and scarf and set off to work.

But on this day her bedroom door was closed and there was only silence. I knew she was there because every now and then I smelled fresh smoke.

At six, when it was way past time for her to leave for work, I tapped on her door, but she didn't answer. I peeked in. She was lying face down on the bed, still in her bathrobe. She turned her head away from me.

"What happened?" I said.

"Nothing."

"Is it something about Paul?"

"No."

"Aren't you going to work?"

"No." After a second she said, "I'm sick."

"Shall I make you tea?"

"No. Close the door."

"What happened? It's about Paul. I know it is."

Viv rose up on her elbows and stared at me like she hated me.

"Close the door, I said."

That night I made grilled tuna fish sandwiches. It was her favorite and I knew she could smell them toasting, but she didn't come out. Finally I ate mine and wrapped hers in foil.

Midnight came but I didn't dare go in for my quilt. Finally I took her raincoat out of the closet and slept under that with her scarf as my pillow.

The next morning I got up and went to school which I thought she would like.

When I got home, she was still in her room. The sandwich was still in its foil and the coffeepot was still upside down in the drainer. Maybe, I thought, she really was sick.

Finally I went in. She was lying on the bed like she'd been before.

"Viv," I said. "Shall I go call a cab and we can go to the emergency room?"

"No."

"What's wrong then? What happened?"

"Nothing. I'm a little sick I told you. Now go on."

"Shall I go and call the Torch Café and tell them you're sick?"

"No. Close the door."

For supper I ate Viv's tuna fish sandwich. There was enough bread left to make her toast if she wanted it, but there wasn't any more to make a sandwiches with. The box of Rice Krispies was maybe a third full and there was half a quart of milk. There were a couple of old pieces of Torch Café steak in foil in the refrigerator. That was about it on food.

In the next days Viv didn't get dressed and I didn't notice that she ate. At the crown of her head brown roots were showing before the golden red started. That was a shock; I always thought the red was real and the stuff she painted on was just to make in shine.

In our apartment, smoke hung like a stinking gray wall and the only sound was her coughing.

By the end of the week we were out of money and Viv was out of cigarettes. She put her coat on over her bathrobe and went out. When she had gone, I raced in to ransack her room; there was nothing in the jewelry box. But in an old handbag at the back of her closet I found an unopened letter. It was in her handwriting, addressed to Paul in Guadalajara, Mexico, and dated the week before Christmas. Across the front was stamped a blue hand with a finger pointing back up at our address. There were a lot of other stamps, all in Spanish. Then somebody had printed in English capital letters, "Refused."

I stopped, afraid that Viv would walk in. I stuck the letter down the back of my pants and put everything back as it had been.

It wasn't until Viv had come back and gone into her room with the carton of cigarettes she'd gotten from somewhere that I took the flashlight out to the garage. I knelt on the floor so that the light couldn't be seen through the window. I got the letter out, opened it carefully so it could be glued back, and read.

"Dearest Paul," Viv had written. "Today I went to the back of the closet for my winter coat. There on the shelf I found the piece of paper with Harry Luck's address in Mexico. I know you left it there for me to find, a few months along, when winter came."

Viv told him she understood how he had been driving himself to build the perfect life, how he began to feel smothered, that it had all become too much for him finally.

"We tried to do what people are supposed to do," she wrote. "But something happened to both of us during the war years and I don't believe either of us will ever be what they call normal. I could feel that you didn't really want the house, the job, the same thing every day. Neither did I! We were both trying to please each other. If we had only just said so!"

She didn't need any of that, she wrote. All she needed was Paul.

I turned off the flashlight and thought about that for a minute. Then I turned the flashlight back on and read the rest, about how she loved him, how she knew she knew he loved her. How she would wait for him forever.

"Now that I have been able to tell you this," she wrote, "I'm happy. I am thinking of you every minute and waiting until I hear from you again."

I switched off the flashlight and knelt in the dark; I tried to think how I felt. The only thing I knew for sure was that Viv would kill me if she found out I knew.

A week or so later, I got caught shoplifting a canned chicken and a carton of Tarrytown Longs at Safeway. The store manager took me in his office and told me he had seen me stealing things for a while now and that he also knew I got produce from the dumpster in back. Now I had better tell him what was going on at home because I didn't look like a bad kid and he didn't want to call the cops.

I said I didn't know what was going on at home, and then we sat there for a long time.

"My mom is sick and can't work," I finally said. "She'll probably be better before long. I'd better go now because she's probably worried about me."

"No," he said. "We have to figure out a plan. Is there anybody who can help you?"

I said there wasn't and he said then he would have to call the authorities because obviously I needed help.

"You don't have anybody else?" he asked.

"No."

"What about your father?"

"No."

"No other relatives? A grandmother or an aunt?"

I shrugged.

"Let's use my phone to call them right now," he said. "We don't have to mention the shoplifting. Tell them what you told me. Your mom is sick and can't work."

Shirley arrived the next afternoon in her pickup. We were both asleep when she knocked on the door of the apartment. She had to keep pounding on the door to get through to us.

When Viv heard the knocking, she came to the door of her room barefoot in her dirty bathrobe, her two-toned hair hanging down.

"It's Shirley," I told her. "It's only Shirley."

Viv turned and went back into her room.

Shirley packed up our household stuff in cardboard boxes she brought in from the back of her pickup. I went out to the garage for the suitcases and stuffed in our clothes.

Viv put on her tan slacks for the first time in weeks; they hung so that you could see she didn't have any behind left. Of course, she hadn't bothered to put on eyebrows. When everything was packed, we all went out and climbed in the cab of Shirley's truck.

"Is the rent paid up?" Shirley asked.

"We haven't paid for a while," I told her. "It's OK. Mrs. Stack doesn't notice. She's too old."

Shirley got out and went and knocked on Mrs. Stack's door.

When she came back, nobody asked if she had settled the rent or what.

"We've got to stop at the post office before we go," Viv said. It was the first thing I'd heard her say in days.

"What for?" Shirley asked.

"To have our mail sent on. I have to fill out an address card."

"We can send a card from the post office at home," Shirley told her. "We'll get home late as it is."

"No," Viv said, her hand on the door handle like she might jump. "Before we go. Then I'll do whatever you want."

So we drove downtown to the post office and Shirley and I waited in the pickup while Viv went in. We sat and watched the people coming in and out of the post office, all of them looking calm and reasonable.

When Viv came back, we drove out through the outskirts of Portland, past Multnomah Falls and then up along the Columbia. The clouds started to drift higher like they always did when you headed east. By the time we got over the Blue Mountains, it was clear and cold; the sky was filled with a million stars. In Portland, you forgot that there *were* stars.

Shirley stopped for gas in Pendleton and went in to pay.

"I got caught shoplifting in Safeway," I told Viv. "The guy said if I didn't have any family to call they'd put us both in jail. That's the only reason."

"It's OK," Viv said. She didn't sound like she cared very much.

"Viv," I dared to say because I could see Shirley, not ten feet from us, coming back from the little office. "What about Chuck?"

Swiftly and with more strength than I could have imagined she still had, Viv pivoted on the seat of the truck and slapped me hard across the face.

And so we came to live with Shirley and Roy; nobody said anything about it being just temporary. Even though Mike had been made to give us his room and had to sleep in the old bunkhouse, he still told me he might let me drive his jeep. He'd built a racetrack for it behind the old mule barn.

"I wouldn't touch that jeep with a ten-foot pole," I said.

Now that we were on the farm we had work to do. After school I was supposed to pitch hay down to the milk cows. I would climb to the loft and kick some hay off the edge to the cows below, but I wasn't going to pick up the fork and pitch. Shirley would have to come up and make me.

So it was a shock, as I stood there kicking, to look down from the loft into the milking parlor below and see Viv, her hair up in a bandana handkerchief, sitting on a little stool. Her forehead rested on the flank of an old cream-colored cow—one of four standing there with their heads in the stanchions—as she expertly squirted milk into a big silver bucket that was already foaming and half-full.

Viv never stopped milking, but she looked up and our eyes met. I couldn't begin to read what I saw.

"'Do your chores,' she said finally. "Chores are good for you," she thought to add.

Then she lowered her eyes and rested her head again on the cow's creamy side.

"I want you both to know what happened to Paul," Shirley came in to say a few nights later when I was washing the supper dishes, another one of my jobs. Mike was there to dry but Viv was not around. Supper over and her work done, she'd be behind the barn, sitting on the ground under the ledge, rolling cigarettes out of the pouch of Drum. Since we hardly had money of our own, that was all she could manage in the way of tobacco.

Shirley stood in the kitchen doorway in her flannel shirt and sock feet. As always when she was serious, she ran her hand through her short dark hair, making it stand up on end.

"He died suddenly of an illness that ran in his family," Shirley said. "If anyone asks, that's what you say. Naturally you and Viv would come back home after something like that. And we're glad to have you."

Shirley waited to see if we had anything to say. I kept washing dishes and Mike kept drying, and Shirley finally turned and went out.

"Shirley said Paul died of an illness that ran in his family," I whispered to Viv when we were getting ready for bed. "Did he?"

We could hear the bedsprings creak in the room next door as Shirley and Roy settled in.

"Yes," Viv finally said.

"When did you hear?"

"A while back."

"Is that why you stopped going to Milo's?" I asked.

"Yes," Viv said after a minute.

"How did you hear?"

"A letter came," Viv said finally.

It was freezing in the bedrooms. Even during the day, when the wood-stove was going in the front room, only a little heat seeped through the walls to the bedrooms. At night when the fire was out, the cold was brutal. In the frozen bed you had to pull yourself up in a ball until the sheets slowly warmed and you could inch your feet down. Luckily there were two of us to generate heat.

Viv and I both turned so our backs were to each other.

"What are we going to do?" I asked. "Are we going to stay here?"

"I don't know," Viv said. "Go to sleep now."

"Are you mad at me? They made me call."

Viv sighed.

"Go to sleep."

"I hate it here. Don't you."

"I don't know," Viv said.

I held my breath and waited but Viv didn't talk any more, maybe already asleep. I dared to edge closer to her, so our backs were just touching.

After that, nobody mentioned Paul and everyone acted like things were settled.

Viv, it turned out, had volunteered to do all the milking as a way of helping pay our way. As a girl, apparently, she'd been especially good at it, fast and thorough, and the cows seemed to like her better than anybody else.

Besides taking over the milking, Viv did all the laundry, once a week wheeling the wringer washer in from the porch to the kitchen, hooking its hose up to the sink, and running four or five loads. She would still be at it when I got home from school, and I helped her hang the leaden sheets in the winter twilight.

I remember seeing her, once, at the other end of a long avenue created by hanging white sheets. She wasn't wearing makeup, of course, and was dressed in Shirley's old jeans and jacket. She'd cut her hair in the bathroom one day, cutting off the ends that were still a goldy red; what was left was an ordinary dishwater brown and she didn't bother to fix it any particular way.

If you squinted your eyes, you might almost think it was Shirley out there in the cold winter light, hauling the heavy sheets up to the high clothesline.

So we went along. I still wouldn't take the chance of liking anything, even Mike's jeep. He'd taken the muffler off, so you had to hear him revving round and round his racetrack. I couldn't keep from hearing—that's probably why he did it—but I wouldn't go and look.

Then things changed a little. Viv began to get visits from a man she had gone all through school with. He was prosperous, that same widowed rancher that Shirley had written about. He lived in a big new house he'd built for his wife and two little boys, down on a pretty acreage along Eagle Creek. Then his wife—also somebody Viv had gone to school with—had been killed in a head-on collision with a logging truck.

He was just about the finest man in the world, according to Shirley.

He came once for supper. After that he came by a couple of times to drive Viv to Bonner to see a movie.

His name was Stan, and if he ever took off his cowboy hat, you saw he was nearly bald. Still he wasn't as much of a cornball as I thought he would be.

"What do you think?" he asked me. "Think it's too tame for Viv out here? After the bright lights of the city?"

I said I didn't know. Maybe.

"What about you?" he asked me. "Found anything you like so far?"

I didn't want to hurt our chances—if this *was* a chance—so I said, I didn't know. Maybe.

"Want a couple of bratty little brothers?"

I shrugged.

"Yeah," he said. "Well, I can't say as I blame you on that one."

All through February Stan came to take Viv out. Waiting for her one night, he asked me if I would like to come over and check out his place and I said OK. He said he had an old motorbike I might like to try. It was too big and fast for the little boys, he said. It was his from when he was about my age.

"OK," I said. I knew he was trying to win me over. Still, I did just glimpse myself riding past our place at sixty miles an hour without even turning my head toward Mike's racetrack.

Then, in mid-March, I came home from school to find Viv in the bathroom, dying her hair the old golden-red color. On the bed in our room were her white suitcases, her hotel dresses neatly packed. The open-toed, high-heeled shoes were wedged into the corners, and scarves and other filmy things blossomed up out of the crevices in the packing. The jeans and boots Viv had worn since we came lay in a pile on the floor.

I went back to the bathroom and stood in the doorway, watching her towel her hair. I could barely breathe.

"I've gotten a job offer," Viv said.

"Where?"

Viv paused for a second.

"California."

"I'll get my suitcase," I said.

But I knew I wasn't going.

At ten-thiry that night—an hour past all of our bedtimes—Shirley went out to warm up the truck. She was driving Viv to Bonner to catch the westbound Greyhound that came through around midnight. Roy had already carried the suitcases out to the pickup and gone to bed and Mike had been sent to the bunkhouse.

Viv came out from the bedroom dressed as if for her hotel job, her hair done up in a smooth, shining roll, her eyebrows flying like wings.

I grabbed both of her shoulders and held on to stop her from leaving. I was almost as strong as she was, and we struggled there in the front room, clenching and pushing.

I got the idea that I should slam her against the stove. Maybe it would go crashing over, break loose from the stovepipe, and fire would rain down. Maybe Viv would be burned and even die. Maybe flames would roar through this rickety old house and within a few minutes we would all be dead and no one would ever be stuck living here anymore.

But then Shirley was at the door, calling my name in her usual quiet way, telling me to let go now and I did.

"I'll write when I'm settled," Viv said. "Then you can come."

She reached for me, but I hit her hands away.

She put on her Portland raincoat and walked out to the truck.

2.

It is not until years later—long after I learned that every time I ran away Shirley would get in her pickup and come find me; long after the adoption papers came for Shirley to sign—that I come across the last letter.

The place is mine now; Shirley and Roy have both been dead for years, neither of them ever quite the same after we lost Mike in Vietnam.

I have my own family; J.P. and I got married when we were still in high school and we have two boys. One of them, Jason, just got married in Portland, and we went down for the wedding. J.P. said do you want to spend the night; he had somebody lined up to milk if I did, but I said, oh, let's just get on home. J.P. said fine by him. He's not much for cities; they're overrated as far as he's concerned. He doesn't know why Jason wants to live down there in all that racket.

Jason told him we're a couple of old stick-in-the-muds, but J.P. said that's fine, there's worse things to be stuck in.

Anyhow, we just climbed in the pickup and drove on home and were glad to get back to these dry old hills.

Jason's wife, though, is a city girl, and she thought it would be cool to have one of Shirley's old P-bar branding irons standing by her fireplace. That's why I'm up here in the hayloft trying to find where those irons got put.

Of course the boys think Shirley was their grandmother and she acted like she was. It was funny to see her go all soft around those little fellows, in a way she never did with Mike or me, good as she was to both to us.

Up here in the loft the floor is rotted in places, so I walk carefully along a wall beam toward the front corner, and yes, there are the branding irons, three of them: long, brutal old things, rusted orange, lying crisscrossed together.

I pry one up out of its nest of pigeon droppings and rotted hay, and am edging back along the wall of the loft when my boot dings on something hard and metal and hollow-sounding. It's a little metal box wedged in under the eaves so that just a corner of it peeks out. I've never noticed it here before, but it's a box I know. Viv used to keep important papers in it when we lived at Mrs. Stack's.

I stand there a minute, the branding iron in my hand.

Some people probably would have just kept on walking. It's getting late, for one thing, and I have to get started on J.P.'s supper.

But I bend down and wedge the box out.

I always knew I would hear from her again.

I blow on the box a few times, making myself cough from the dust. The box is closed with a cheap little lock, but one good smash from the branding iron pops it open.

Inside there's only one envelope. It's in Paul's hand, addressed to Viv in Portland and forwarded here. The return address is Los Angeles, California and it's dated March, 1956.

I take the soft old envelope out of the metal box and walk back along the beam to the high loft window.

Evening's coming on fast, but there's still just enough light to see.

I shake the letter out.

"Dearest Viv," it begins, "a letter from my buddy Harry Luck just caught up with me here in LA. He says you wrote to me down in Guadalajara a while back. He opened your letter by mistake; when he saw it wasn't for him, he sealed it back up and returned it. At first, he felt bad for opening it. Then he got to thinking about what it had said and he started feeling bad that he sent it back."

Paul wrote that Harry had tracked him down through some other buddies and had written Paul a letter, asking him why he was such a jackass and a dope. Harry also wanted to know why he should have bothered patching Paul up in '43 if this was the best he could do, running out when he finally got a great girl like Viv.

Paul said that he hadn't dared to contact Viv after what he'd done. He'd felt sure she hated his guts by now. But with Harry behind him—and knowing she had tried to reach him—he would try, hoping against hope.

He left, he said, because he felt overwhelmed with fear. The harder he tried to build the right kind of life, the more the fear would close in.

"Right before I left," Paul wrote, "I actually went blind for a few minutes. I remember being alone in our little apartment and suddenly I was looking down a long black tunnel. Then even that light was gone and I couldn't see my hand. I felt my way to the bathroom to put my head under the tap until my vision gradually returned. When these types of feelings came over me, I was afraid I was cracking up again, and the only thing I knew to do was run."

There's more but the light is fading. I glance through the letter to the last paragraph where Paul asks Viv if she remembers that movie where Lauren Bacall stands by Humphrey Bogart.

"In the final scene," Paul writes, "he's in some beachfront bar. He's sitting there, and you think he's all alone, just this lonely sad guy. But then he happens to look up and there she is. She's one of those girls who will believe in her guy and wait for him forever."

I fold the letter up and put it back in the envelope. I put the envelope back in the little metal box.

I stand in the high barn window for a minute and look out over my place. It's nearly dark down below, but the high mountains that guard the valley to the west glow blue-white, as if illuminated, still, by the sun that has gone down behind them.

I watch the mountains change from blue-white to pale blue. Soon they will shade into a deep dark violet. But I can't stand here and watch. If I don't go now it will be too dark to see my way.

So I turn my back on the mountains and edge along the beam, into the dark loft; I put the little box in the same spot under the eaves. I kick it once, twice, three times, so it wedges in, all but invisible. Now, going completely by feel, I find the ladder nailed to the wall. I climb down into the inky black barn.

Roll

His jaw had been twitching for fifty miles so she wasn't too surprised when all of a sudden he yanked the steering wheel to one side. The pickup veered off the narrow dirt road and went jolting along through the sagebrush, coming to a stop at the canyon edge. Below, she knew, was the long, rocky, and only slightly slanted drop to the river. She couldn't see down into the canyon just then, because the pickup had come to rest with its nose pointed up. All she could see was big flat sky.

She wouldn't be surprised if one of the tires was half off. She had seen him pull this stunt before, hang a part of the tire off the canyon edge. Just showing off. These other times, though, he'd told her to get out first so nobody would get killed but possibly him.

She'd imagined it. Probably you wouldn't shoot straight down and explode. Probably you would roll, maybe in a kind of slow motion. The pickup didn't have seat belts so you'd just have to hold on. Maybe you could even drop down into the space beneath the glove compartment and brace yourself there to keep from flying out and getting crushed.

On the driver's side there was no such little pocket, and she remembered hearing of somebody impaled on his steering wheel.

If you made it to the bottom of the canyon alive, of course, you'd have to climb back up on your own. There weren't more than one or two cars or trucks along this road a day, and anyway who'd look down? Unless there was smoke or something.

They sat there on the edge. She knew he would grab her if she tried to jump out. And that much of a jostle might be all it would take to send them over.

If they started to tip, at least, he'd have to hang on and couldn't get to her; then she'd drop down to her little space under the dash.

They sat and waited to see what would happen next. Barely breathing, she watched herself in the side mirror, as if staring into her own eyes would keep her alive.

After a while he threw it in reverse. The wheels spun and for a second or two it seemed that they weren't going to have enough traction. This was what she was maybe scared of most, that even if he didn't exactly mean to get them both killed, he'd go too far and then couldn't get back. Like maybe he wasn't as smart as he thought.

But then she felt the tires catch hold, and the truck went bouncing backwards over the sagebrush and onto the road again.

It took them an hour to get through the canyon and come out at the town of Bonner. This was the last chance to get gas before heading out home, and he stopped at a filling station. While he was in paying, she took her handbag and got out of the truck. She walked around to the ladies' bathroom at the side. She limped a little like her foot hurt and she couldn't walk fast. When she got around the corner, she tucked her handbag under her arm and sprinted, across a street, through a yard, over a fence, through a hedge. She ran through one yard and then another one and still one more. Noticing a porch with a crawl space underneath, she hit the ground and rolled under, edging along on her back until she was up against the cool foundation of the house.

Panting, she looked around to see if there was anything in there a dog might have drug in, because if there was a dog he would find her and start barking. But there weren't any bones or balls or filthy old rags. It was a nice clean crawl space, hard clean dirt.

She stayed there until night, lying on her back and breathing, relaxing all parts of her body and noticing that nothing was broken or even hurt. She felt nervous for an hour or so because what if somebody from one of the houses had seen her run by and was out tracking her down. But after a while, it seemed that if anybody had seen her, they would have found her by now so she stopped worrying about that.

Was he going around pounding on doors and telling people they'd better cough her up if she was hiding there? She thought and decided, no. He didn't like to talk to people as much as that. Probably he was parked somewhere, waiting for her to be dumb enough to walk by.

The ground was hard but she had her handbag under her head for a pillow. There were a few bugs that crawled on her arms from time to time. They were just little ants. She wished she had a cracker or something so she could put out a crumb and pass the time watching them try to pick it up and carry it off. She always loved seeing a little tiny ant carry off a crumb ten times its size. Yeah, except if she had a cracker she'd eat it herself. Breakfast seemed like about a year ago.

It was quiet under there. Bonner was the county seat and a good-sized town, so there were cars and the occasional horn honking, but it was still pretty quiet. There wasn't any sound coming from the house above, nobody thumping and stomping around. There was no sound of sirens or anything. The last thing he would do would be call the police, of course.

It got dark and she couldn't see a thing. In the blackness, she started worrying again. Thinking maybe she should have run farther. Thinking how she was only one block over from the gas station. Now that it was dark, she began to imagine him circling around through the quiet, little streets, hoping to see somebody go racing through the headlights.

He would really kill her this time, she wouldn't be surprised.

If she had a watch she would check the time, since, as most people knew, the Portland bus came through Bonner at 11:23 p.m. At that time, it might be fair to guess, he would be over watching for her at the Antler's Hotel where the bus stopped. That might have been a good moment to creep farther away from the gas station. That's what she would have done if she'd had a watch and knew when that exact moment had come.

It wasn't cold and she slept some. The main problem was the ants; they'd all found her now.

What about the milking, she remembered when she woke up once. Didn't he have to go home to milk? She didn't know exactly what happened if you skipped milking, but she knew it was bad. The cows got sick, she thought. She'd never known him not to milk. Remembering that, she turned over and got a little more comfortable.

The morning light began to seep in and she started to wonder whose house this probably was anyway. They were awful quiet, whoever they were. Or maybe not. Maybe there were ten of them making a big racket, and you just couldn't hear from down here.

She smiled to think of them all up there not knowing that someone had crawled in under their back porch.

The light came on and it got warmer. She was glad for that anyhow.

Yeah, unless he was out there waiting for daylight, figuring she'd come popping out, like a little field mouse, dumb enough to stick its head up out of its hole.

You should have tried to get farther from the gas station when it was dark, instead of just lying here, she told herself.

You never think, she said to herself. All you do is try to get by and you don't think. That's what you are like.

Yes, she said. Yes, I am like that mostly. But I got out and ran, didn't I.

Well, yes, she replied to herself. Yes, you did. Took you long enough.

Now there was a sound, a scraping, shuffling sound on the porch above. Maybe it was an old person or someone who was sick. That would be good if it was only one old sick person up there.

"Penny!" the person up there on the porch called out in an old man's voice, "Penny!"

Strange to be calling out for a penny.

Well, of course, it was probably a name. Like a dog's name. Maybe the dog had been in the house all this time, but would now come out sniffing around and find her.

She grabbed her handbag and listened. But there was no click-click-click of dog toenails on the boards above. There were only more shuffling and scraping sounds that could have been someone pulling up a chair to sit in. Yes, it sounded like he'd pulled up a chair and was sitting right over her head.

"Penny!" he called out every now and then, and there'd be more shuffling.

She had to go to the bathroom really bad now and the ants were beginning to drive her crazy. And it looked like this old guy was going to sit there calling out Penny all day.

She put her handbag under her elbow, turned on her stomach, and crawled forward. She turned sideways and rolled out from under the porch. And, yes, there he was looking right at her, a big old guy in a VFW cap with a bunch of badges and buttons pinned to it. He sat in a wheelchair with crutches propped beside it, and one of his feet was missing. He had a cat on his lap that he was petting, so OK that was Penny.

She stood up and brushed herself off.

"Could I use your bathroom, please," she said. "My car wrecked and I had to sleep somewhere. I hope you didn't mind. I would have asked but it was late."

She hadn't planned to say any of this and was surprised to hear all that come out.

Pretty good there, she said to herself.

He looked at her. He seemed to see her but not to get what she was saying.

"Could I use your bathroom, please," she said, louder but not wanting to yell.

He didn't say yes, but he didn't say no either. He seemed to have just gone back to petting his cat. So she dusted herself some more and came up on the porch.

"Hi," she said when she got up there, but he didn't even look in her direction.

So she went on in the back door.

The kitchen wasn't as bad as you would think. Kind of smelly, of course, like the usual man's house. Old-fashioned; nobody had put in a new stove or sink for about fifty years. But it wasn't a horrible jumbled rotting mess like other crazy old people's houses she'd seen. There were dirty dishes in the sink, but not, like, a month's worth.

She found the bathroom off the kitchen and used the toilet that wasn't too disgusting. She washed her hands and face in the sink. There was a towel that wasn't too bad and the shower when she turned it on had hot water, so she stripped off her clothes and got in. She even washed her hair with some shampoo that was there.

I'm smarter than he thinks, she told herself. Here I am, still alive and even taking a shower.

While she was standing there in the water, she heard talking, and by its regular nature she realized it was a radio that someone had just turned on.

Somebody else is here, she said to herself. Moron.

When she came out of the bathroom, there the other person was, a young guy, kind of fat, barefoot and wearing an ugly yellow sweat suit. He had pretty, coppery hair though. When he saw her, he snapped off the radio.

"Who are you?" he said.

"Oh. I had a car wreck."

"In our bathroom?"

She laughed.

"Out on the road. It was late, and I just kind of crawled away. I think I was nearly unconscious or something. When I woke up I was under your porch so I asked that old guy if I could use the bathroom. He said I could."

"Where's your car now?"

"Well. I'm not sure. It must be around here somewhere. You know, I was, like, in a coma."

He reached in the kitchen drawer and took out a little black gun.

"Got any idea how long I've been waiting to use this?" he asked. "In this hick town?"

"I bet. Yeah. But don't worry, I'll just leave. I only wanted to use the bathroom and that old guy was nice enough to say I could."

"He didn't say you could. He wouldn't understand something like that."

"Poor old soul. Is he a veteran?"

"Yeah. He's a war hero, matter of fact. Purple Heart."

"Oh wow."

"So why did you say he said you could use the bathroom when he didn't?"

"I thought he kind of nodded like it would be OK. He didn't say no. And you know, most people are nice enough to let you use their bathroom. So I assumed it would be OK. I'm sorry if it wasn't."

"I heard you taking a shower."

"Yeah, I don't even know why I did that. I'm still kind of woozy I think. Could I have a glass of water? Then I can just go."

"You're not going anywhere."

"The thing is my husband is going to kill me for this. I mean really kill me dead. You don't want him to find me here. He's gone crazy I think."

"I'm not scared of your nut job of a husband."

She could see he wasn't. He did have the gun.

"Could I please have a drink of water."

He nodded and she went over to the sink and got herself a cup of water from the tap. It was sweet and cold.

"I'm an ex-con," he said. "What do you think of that?"

"What for," she said. "Drugs? Like weed or something?"

He laughed a little. Not in a mean way. More like, yeah, you got that right.

"What's your game anyhow," he said. He scratched his lip with the butt of the gun like he'd forgotten what it even was.

"Penny!" the old guy out on the porch suddenly called out. "Penny!"

"Who's Penny?" she asked. "The cat?"

"No. The cat's name is Ace."

"Oh. I figured he was calling his cat."

"No. He's calling me. My name's Penny."

"Oh. Hi. Mine's Joleen."

"Hi," he said. "You don't really have a husband do you?"

"Yes, I do. And he's gone berserk. He almost rolled his truck over the Schmidt Grade on purpose so we'd both get killed. When he stopped at that gas station over there I ran. I wasn't really in a car wreck."

She took a deep breath.

"Maybe I shouldn't have told you that."

"He's from here?"

"From out near Pine. He's a farmer."

The guy laughed again.

"Well. I thought a farmer would be nice."

The guy made a face like, yeah, sure, good old farmers.

"I thought it would be healthy. No, like, bars to go to. Hardly. We do have one tavern out there. But it closes at nine. And he gets up so early to milk. I've been living out there for six months and he hasn't missed milking once.

"He picked me up hitchhiking," she added. "I know you shouldn't meet people that way. You should meet people in more of a family setting."

Penny put the gun back in the drawer. He opened a cabinet beside the stove and took out a big black frying pan. He put it on the burner and lit the gas underneath with a match, then went over to the refrigerator and got out a package of bacon and a carton of eggs. He rummaged around on the bottom shelf of the refrigerator until he came up with a loaf of bread.

She stayed where she was next to the sink. Already you could smell the frying pan getting hot. Penny peeled off five or six strips of bacon and laid them side by side. In a minute the fine fat bacon smell rose up to fill the room. He took a fork and turned each strip over.

"Penny!" the old guy yelled.

"Keep your pants on, Grandpa!" Penny went to kitchen door to yell. "I'm up."

He poured some orange drink from a carton in the fridge and took it out to the old guy.

While he was gone, Joleen crossed over and got plates from the cup-board. She put two of them on the kitchen table. She figured two could mean the grandpa and Penny or it could mean Penny and her because maybe the old man would eat out in his chair. Penny could take it the way he wanted.

She got knives and forks and put them beside the plate and then for a little nice touch she folded paper towels lengthways to be napkins.

Penny came back in and glanced at the table but didn't say anything.

He lifted the strips of bacon out of the frying pan and put them on a plate to drain then poured most of the bacon grease into the sink. He took eggs and cracked them one handed, two at a time into the sizzling pan. He cracked six in all.

"Hungry?" he said.

Yukon River

It's mostly drunk Indians where I'm working at the moment. Better than mostly white guys. Indians just drink. White guys, it's got to be you *look* like somebody.

One night this guy Len shows up; he's stopping in Seattle to get some final stuff before heading to Alaska. He's going to settle on some land he bought, out in the bush, way up the Yukon River. He doesn't think I look like anybody but he wants me to come with him.

Every night he waits for me in the Doughnut Hole two doors down. It's a dump and nobody's ever there but him and a bum lady, Irene. Irene tells Len things she has learned from messages coded into license plates of cars that go by on First Avenue. She tells him he was burned at the stake in a previous life so not to worry about *that* again. He should watch out for green death rays though. Don't worry about the other colors, Irene says. Len frowns, listening carefully so that Irene won't feel bad.

In the dead white light of the Hole, Irene looks like she's a hundred. But if you look close, you see she's not all that old. Forty maybe. Maybe less. Maybe a beat-up thirty-five, even. I'm twenty-nine so I probably look about sixty.

Len, though, with his clear, bright eyes and his long, soft, gently waving hair, is always beautiful, no matter the light. My first thought was: he's too good for me. My second thought: I know him from somewhere. My third thought: he looks exactly like the picture of Jesus Grandma used to keep on the piano.

Len is beautiful despite no-good parents and bad foster homes and even a stint in prison. In fact, it was on a top bunk in the never-ending roar of the California State Prison at Folsom that he started reading about Alaska, going every night into its immense and perfect silence. He read everything there was on Alaska. Then he got an idea. Go there really. Go someplace where you can make up your own life. Where nothing is ugly. Where there's nobody else to screw things up. Go someplace that's the opposite of prison.

When he got out he did a few big but careful drug deals to fund the Alaska thing. When he had the money, he read the advertisements and finally found somebody with land to sell. Once he'd closed the deal, he had enough left over for a truck and other gear. Now, he's finished with all that drug stuff forever. He won't need it anymore.

He looks at me, wide-eyed with wonder and belief.

It was the final drug deals that sold me on going along with him; I'm not sure why. Just, I guess, it's not all magic.

"What will we do," I ask, "once we were are out there?"

Len can tell me because he knows everything about subsistence life in the bush. He knows how we'll pull salmon out of the river, cut them in strips, brine them and dry them. How those pickled salmon strips will eat like candy all winter. He knows how we'll collect berries in the hills around our place—blueberries, blackberries, salmon berries, all in unbelievable abundance—and make them into jam and pies and berry bread. He knows how in the summer we'll float the gleaming river at midnight, and how in the winter we'll sleep tight and warm as goslings in our good-to-fifty-below goose-down bags.

He knows how we'll build a log sauna, and how we'll sit there together, glowing and cleansing during even the longest and darkest nights.

He knows too that this isn't really my question.

"What do you do anywhere?" he asks back, looking so deeply into me that I shiver. "What do you do here?"

We leave Seattle and drive up the Alcan Highway in the big pickup truck Len has outfitted for the Arctic. He's from California; I'm from all over. Neither of us has ever been in really cold country, but he's read everything about surviving in the cold, keeping your truck running and so forth. He's got everything planned and most things we'll need are packed in a carrier on the roof.

It's February and it's still cold, around fifteen below, as we drive north through British Columbia and then into the Yukon Territory. When we have to get out of the truck to gas up or take a pee, the cold washes effortlessly through the soles of our boots. It freezes the hairs in our noses; it freezes our eyelashes.

We take turns driving until we are both exhausted, then pull off to the side. We climb in back and heat canned stew on the little kerosene stove; we eat it out of our big tin cups. Then we sleep close and tight in our zipped-together bags.

Len loves the power of this cold. The cold, he says, purifies everything, killing all the putrid crap. It is purifying us. He can feel it.

Do I feel it? Maybe.

We drive north. The sky pales and expands; the trees shrink and the landscape empties. The sun must be somewhere, but I don't see it. It seems that we are driving along on Mars.

We are tired and stiff from long days in the truck. Yet we are happy and in perfect harmony. We are already becoming free, Len says. See?

I just look at him. Whatever it is he's figured out, I want to know too.

We drive north. We cross into Alaska from the Yukon. Now the truck's heater can't keep up with the cold, and we bring the sleeping bags up to the cab to drape over us as we drive. We keep the water bottle in the cab so it won't freeze. At night, we put the bottle in bed with us to keep it warm so we'll have water for coffee in the morning.

One morning the truck won't start and I'm scared. We are alone in the middle of frozen nowhere; it seems that if something goes wrong, it wouldn't take long to die. But Len has read up on what to do if this happens. He gets out his little Primus camp stove, fires it up, and rolls under the truck to position the stove beneath the oil pan. In fifteen minutes the truck catches hold.

Len smiles the wondering smile of a six-year-old genius.

"Doubt if you'll find a place to stay," a service station guy in an insulated jumpsuit tells us when we finally and triumphantly hit Fairbanks. People are still flooding in to work on the pipeline, he says; they come in from the airport by the busload, even though most of them don't have a prayer of a job. Too, the pipeline companies have grabbed up most of the apartments and motel rooms for their own big shots.

"You're probably thinking campground," the guy says, glancing out at our truck. But the campgrounds are full, even now, he tells us. Everything that can be divided up already has been; people even started dividing their trailer houses up into three or four cubicles.

"This one lady in the paper," the guy says. "She rented out the space between her washer and dryer for somebody to sleep in."

The guy says he's tired of it and he's going back down to Minnesota when he gets the money for a plane ticket.

"It's mostly guys from Texas and Oklahoma that get the pipeline jobs," he tells us. "They've got it all fixed with their union. If you're not one of their boys, forget it."

We pull out into the clogged traffic of Airport Way. It's trucks mostly, everything stop-and-go, everybody pumping out exhaust that freezes into a fog. The snow that edges the roads is a filthy gray.

It's 1975, and Len had known about the pipeline. But he thought it would be far away, lost in the immense space of Alaska, a little trickle of silver sliding alone silently in the vast slope of snow. He had not thought of it being right here, a fat ugly snake of greed and pollution; he had not imagined it strangling the little snow-covered log-cabin town he had fallen in love with as he lay on his bunk in Folsom.

We battle the traffic until we get out of town and can pull over onto a bare piece of ground.

We sit for a while, our engine running, pumping our own frozen exhaust into the air. I look for myself in the side-view mirror but everything is frozen and fogged and I'm nowhere to be seen.

Len thinks for a long time. Then he turns to me and smiles his Jesus smile.

"Good," he says. "Now we see why we have to go out to our land."

It looks for a while like we might have to sleep in the truck until spring. Then a guy who manages a hardware store tells us that for three hundred a month we can set up a tent alongside his cabin out on Chena Hot Springs Road. Since we don't have a tent, the guy says for another couple hundred he can rent us a double-sided tent he has along with the insulation to go between the walls. He can rent us flooring and a chunk of carpet to help hold the heat. We have one woodstove with us, but the guy in the store— X-Man he says his name is—convinces Len that since it's a tent we need two woodstoves, one at each end. The guy rents us the extra stove for fifty a month. Len tries to give him a check on his California bank, but X-Man says, that's all right, he can carry us until we go to the bank and get cash.

X-Man says he guesses he knows where we live. Len laughs and puts his checkbook back in his pack.

X-Man says, too, the interest rate up here for loans is ten percent a month, what with all the coming and going. He's got to remember he's a businessman, he says, much as he'd rather just help us out.

Len smiles his Jesus smile.

"Sure," he says.

The hardware store is warm, and there are rocking chairs in back beside the stove. It's nice to sit in a chair after so long on the road; we both kind of go into a trance. We sit there for a couple of hours. When X-Man isn't waiting on customers, he comes back and talks. He's a big guy and a big talker and he seems glad to have us sit there and listen. He's a native Alaskan, he tells us; his great-grandfather was a Klondiker in 1898, one of the few to make it on foot over the White Pass Trail with his hundred pounds of supplies. Most people fell by the wayside, he tells us. Thousands of men either gave up or died or sometimes went insane, it was so bad.

X-Man goes on to tell us we don't know how lucky we are to actually have land. Everybody in Alaska wants land, he says, even people who've lived their whole lives here, people you would think had a right. But no such thing, X-Man says. The Feds own it all. Do we realize what percentage of Alaska is owned by actual people, not counting Natives? One percent. And why is that? Why can't people get land to live on? Why don't they open it back up to homesteading like in the old days, when America was really America?

We don't know. X-Man says he sure as hell doesn't know either.

Why Alaska ever wanted to be part of the United States, he says, is beyond him. If people would get off their rears, maybe they could get up a secession movement. But people just don't have that much balls. Balls, he says, went out in the old days.

Len shrugs and smiles

X-Man smiles too and stops ranting about everything.

"I'm glad you're here, man," X-Man says. "You and your lady."

He winks at me.

"Hard to keep a good lady up here," he says.

●

The next day we go out to where X-Man lives and set up our tent next to his little house. It's hard working in the cold; despite thick gloves, we don't have long until our hands start to freeze and we have to get back in the truck with the heater on. Len hates to sit in the truck with the exhaust pumping out into the environment, but neither of us can do anything with our hands frozen. Neither of us is big, but we are both pretty strong in a stringy, little-person way and we work well together setting all this stuff up. Once we get the floorboards set and the outer tent up, we come inside, light a kerosene lantern, and start putting up the slabs of insulation. Then it's not too hard to set up the inner tent. We set up the woodstoves and work the stovepipe out through the holes already cut in the tent canvas. We bring in some of the wood we bought from X-Man and get a fire going.

We put up folding chairs and a folding table that Len had packed on top of the truck. We get out the teakettle and put it on the stove. The tent starts to get a little warm and the water in the kettle even boils; then here we are sitting at our table drinking tea.

Len smiles.

"See?" he says.

X-Man comes by when he gets home from work.

"Pretty good," he says looking around.

We all sit by the stove and drink tea.

X-Man says he still can't believe how lucky we are to actually own land in the bush. He just thinks we are so darn lucky

He says he sure hopes the land we bought is one of the old homesteads that people really have title to. These days, he says, lots of people think they've got land to buy and sell. Turns out it's usually federal land and nobody has a right to it. Sooner or later, the BLM'll find you and throw you off, no matter how hidden in the bush you think you are.

Those BLM guys are mother-fuckers, X-Man says; you don't leave that very minute, they burn your cabin and shoot your dogs.

He sits and shakes his head over the badness of the BLM.

Len pours more tea.

X-Man tells us more Alaska stories. He tells a story of this woman living out in the bush who went crazy and started building a wooden walkway that began at her cabin and then just headed nowhere. All she would do was work on that walkway, even though she was about two hundred miles from anywhere.

"Lots of people go crazy out there," X-Man says.

"Lots of people go crazy lots of places," Len says, smiling.

Is our place an old homestead, I ask when X-Man is gone. Len says yes; he's got the original papers from the 1960s to prove it. He says he'll dig them out and show me if I want.

I say no that's OK. If he's sure.

"I'm sure," he says. "But I would go anyway. Even if I weren't."

We settle in to wait for the spring thaw, "breakup" they call it. Just about all we have to do is wait and Len is happy waiting. He can sit beside the stove all day, drinking tea and poring over the plans that he has laid out on the little table, studying up on how to build a nice, tight cabin out of three-sided logs. There's an old cabin up there now, Len tells me; but it's probably pretty dilapidated. We'll need something better by winter.

He sits all day in the light from the kerosene lamp, studying things. He loves all the lore about how to live in the bush. He especially loves an article he has about how to set nets under the frozen surface of a river to catch fish year-round.

"Just think," he says. "Under all that ice, they're having a gay old time."

It's late February now, and every day there's more light. If it's getting warmer, though, it's hard to tell.

"Be careful," X-Man tells us on one of his visits to the tent. "When it goes up to ten below after it's been forty below, you think it's warm."

That's a good way to freeze to death, he tells us.

"It happens to newcomers every spring," he says. "Just because it's not as bad as it was, you think it isn't bad. But it is."

"That guy," Len says when he's gone. "He thinks he knows what bad is."

However bad or not bad the cold is, we are fairly warm in our double-sided tent. During the day we keep the fire going in the two stoves. At night we let one stove go out and just keep a fire in the airtight. It's a good stove because it will hold a fire all night. Because it's so efficient, it doesn't pollute too much.

We spend a lot of time in bed, snuggling in the goose-down bags. We cuddle and screw. Len dreams out loud of our place on the river. How the water will gently gleam in the soft white Arctic light, how the nights will glow and the stars will dance. How tired and innocent and good we will be when, after our long days of fishing and berry-picking and water-hauling, we come in, finally, to the warm lamplight.

"Don't be afraid of X-Man," he whispers in my ear. "I've known a hundred X-Men."

Then, as if drugged by his dreams, Len drops into a deep sleep, barely moving for ten or twelve hours.

I can't sleep the long hours he can. Sometimes I light a lantern and just lie there, warm in goose down, watching him sleep. With his shining eyes closed, he looks different. Smaller. Older. Worried. This, I guess, is the part of him left over from prison.

Len has never asked me for anything, never said anything about me kicking in some cash. And I've never asked him how much money he has. He's careful what he spends though, and I worry it could cost more than he thinks to get out of Fairbanks and up to the land.

"Why don't I see if I can pick up work," I tell him after a week. "While we're waiting. Might as well pull in a few bucks."

He looks up from the book he is studying. It's a book about geodesic domes. Seeing how well this double-sided tent works, he's wondering if, instead of the log house he has planned, he could maybe build a double-sided dome with foot-thick insulation between the sides. X-Man has been telling him how expensive it will be to have the three-sided logs floated in on the river. And how, what with the pipeline, you can't hire people to do things even if you can pay.

Len looks at me like he sometimes does, like he is seeing me there for the first time and is surprised, thinking: Wow, who is this great girl standing here?

"OK," he says. "Good."

"Len," I say. "You are the most beautiful person I've ever known."

He smiles and dips his head a little, like, yeah, I can't help it.

•

It's not hard to get on waitressing at a steak house on the dinner shift. It's a hassle driving to the restaurant on the clogged roads, and sometimes when the ice fog is especially thick I feel like I'm driving blind; I expect a pipeline truck to plow into me any minute. But when I get to the restaurant it's warm and bright. The salary is good, and the tips are the best I've ever seen.

It's true this place is up to its neck in money, and money seems to be all anybody can talk about. Up on the pipeline, it doesn't matter if you are an engineer or a cook or what, you can make thousands a month. So people say. Your room and board are free and all you eat is steak and lobster.

Just about everybody is trying to figure how to get on the line somehow.

The other girls working at the restaurant are friendly enough but rowdy. All of them are from someplace else—Texas and Oklahoma, lots of them—and they've all come up with boyfriends or husbands who are out on the line. All of their boyfriends or husbands are trying to get them on as chambermaids or cooks' helpers. Anything. It doesn't matter; it's big money no matter what you do.

In the kitchen they all yak about their plans for being Alaska-rich when they get home. It appears they all want a split-level house with a swimming pool. Their husbands are going to set up in business, and they are going to have kids and be the foxiest PTA moms ever. They'll make all the moms who've never been out of Tulsa just burn.

We have the best steaks in Fairbanks—so we claim anyhow—and now and then we get a guy that the girls will peg as a pimp. One of them, Harold, takes a big interest in us waitresses. He's plump and black and shows up most nights for dinner. He's always laughing a big pink laugh and always hinting that for classy girls like us there are better ways to make money than waitressing.

In the kitchen everybody laughs and screams about who will be first to take Harold up on his offer. Maybe it would be fun, they say. For a little while. Just until their husbands come down from the line. Maybe it would be an adventure before going home.

Harold seems pretty small-time, but there's one guy who comes swishing in around ten like he owns the place. He's dark and flashy and for a second I think I know him from somewhere, Reno maybe. But up close I see he's not the guy I'm thinking of; this guy's wearing his own hair, for one thing.

He wears a white shirt and tie under a wolf-fur parka, and he keeps his money in a clip that he leaves on the table while he eats. When he's ready to pay, he rolls a hundred dollar bill off the top and you can see all the hundreds underneath.

The girls don't want to wait on him because they think he's wearing eyeliner and they can't stand queers.

I wait on him because he tips better than anybody. Anyway, I doubt being queer is the worst thing about him. The girls who come in with him look way too young, for one thing.

His drink is a White Russian and every time he orders, he asks me to sniff the cream they use in the bar to make sure it's fresh. He adds five dollars to the tip just for that. I say I will sniff the cream, but I don't. I let him take his chances.

It's a fairly nice restaurant, but like all restaurants, it stinks. The kitchen stinks of grease and food rotting in places you can't reach to clean. In the bar, you smell all the booze that's been spilled on the floor since the Gold Rush probably. The ashtrays of course stink and even the clean napkins smell of a thousand people wiping their mouths. The carpets are always filthy, though we vacuum them every night. I breathe it all in and think of the land we are going to, so pure, so clean, so crudless.

When I get home I take water from the teakettle and fill a basin; I sponge myself all over so Len doesn't have to smell the dirty restaurant on me.

X-Man is always dropping by. Len is nice to him, but I notice that his face gets the old, small look when X-Man is there.

"You're just plain lucky," X-Man keeps telling us.

"Some people got all the luck," he says. "That's all there is to it. Let's just hope that land of yours is good."

"It's good," Len says.

X-Man says he bets it is. He sure does *hope* it is. He shakes his head and laughs.

"What's funny," I ask him.

"Oh," he says. "Nothing. I was just thinking about this guy who was up last spring."

"What about him?"

X-Man says, oh, it's just a story about a guy who came up from somewhere. Arizona or somewhere. X-Man got to know the guy because he was always hanging around the store. Anyhow, breakup came, and this guy loaded all his stuff in a boat and went out to some land he had title to. Come to think of it, this guy had *two* boats; he had his sled dogs with him, so they had to go in their own boat.

"Are you taking dogs?" he interrupts himself to ask.

Len says he'll see.

Anyhow, X-Man says, this guy landed somewhere way up on the Porcupine River. One of the boats was a motorboat and it was pulling the second boat that had the dogs in it. The guy had to figure out how to tie the dogs in, so they wouldn't get away.

"That must have been quite a sight," X-Man says. "Must have looked like Noah's Ark."

He laughs to think of it.

Long story short, he says, when this guy got to his land, where it had been described to him to be, he nosed his boat in and jumped off.

"What do you think happened?" X-Man asks us.

"The dogs got untied and ran off?" I guess.

"Worse 'n that. Oh, much worse 'n that."

Neither of us asks him what happened.

"What happened," X-man says, "is that the guy jumped off his boat and he sank up to mid-thigh. Nothing there but marsh. He tried wading but there wasn't nothing to wade *to*."

"What did he do?" I ask.

X-Man shakes his head.

"Nothing to do but come back. And I believe, come to think of it, he *did* lose the dogs on the way back down. Boy, that guy was busted when he got back."

We sit there and drink tea and wish he would go away.

How did Len manage to get his hands on the land, X-Man wants to know.

Len says it was just one of those things.

"Where's it at?" X-Man asks.

"It's on the Yukon," Len says. "North of Circle City. We'll put in the river there at Circle. Just as soon as the road opens up."

"You got it on the map?" X-Man asks.

Len gets out one of his maps and puts a little pencil dot where our land is.

X-Man takes the map. He pushes his glasses up on his forehead and looks hard at the little dot. He measures how far it is from Circle with his finger. He asks us who the guy was we bought it from. Len says it was somebody he met in California.

"California," X-Man laughs. "Probably couldn't stick it up here."

"Could be," Len says.

X-Man says that sounds real believable because it's only a certain type of person who can make it in the bush. He tells a story about a couple of guys who'd been out there too long and started thinking a Sasquatch was prowling around their place. One of the guys got so freaked he ended up shooting his buddy by mistake. Shot him dead. Tried to hide it and ended up in prison.

"You're taking guns, I suppose," X-Man says.

Len smiles.

"Sure. Want to see my guns?"

But X-Man doesn't want to see them.

"I didn't know you had guns," I say when X-Man is gone.

Len smiles and shrugs like Jesus would shrug if he didn't want to talk about whether he had guns or not.

The guy who may or may not be wearing eyeliner knows to sit in my section. He's not friendly and doesn't want to chat, but he does let me know that he has a strip club out on the Old Richardson Highway. The strippers there are professionals he tells me. Only the best. He flies them up from Vegas.

He gives me a look like don't even think you could be a stripper.

On the other hand, he tells me, he's always looking for local talent as dancers. It's just regular girls. Not too fat. Not too short.

He nods toward the girls he's got with him. They eat and don't say anything. They are not too fat or too short, I guess, is the point.

All you do is dance in a T-shirt and hot pants up on a stage, the guy says. There's a couple of bouncers and nobody gets close. Afterward you can walk around for tips.

He gives me his card with his personal telephone number handwritten on the back in case I decide to try out dancing.

The girls watch me to see if I turn it over to look at the number.

Supposedly spring is coming.

"Careful," X-Man drops in to warn. "Spring is when most people commit suicide. I never heard why. Maybe they get their hopes up too much."

Even though spring is coming, the bowl Fairbanks sits in is still filled up with ice fog. It seems like the fog is getting, if possible, thicker. Coming back from the restaurant one night, I lose the road and end up on an abandoned train track. I have to hitch a ride home. The next day we hitch back to get the truck loose. But it's stuck between the ties and Len says we'll need a tow truck.

"Oh, you won't get a tow truck inside six weeks," X-Man says when we ask him if he knows anybody. "If that. They're all up on the line."

X-Man gets a laugh out of it.

"Guess you won't be going anywhere anytime soon," he says.

Len and I hitch back out. We dig and push and spin the wheels for half a day and don't look at each other. Finally a couple of guys stop. They have a winch on the front of their rig. They hook up to us and we push from the back and finally manage to lurch the truck up over the ties.

Len has his little stove and he crawls under the truck with it to thaw out the oil pan.

Overhead, I notice, are Northern Lights, the first I've seen, dancing all crazy colors.

Len comes out to look.

"Would you call any of that green?" he asks.

"No," I say. "I would call it blue and white."

X-Man's rig is there when we get back and his lights are on. He doesn't come out to congratulate us on getting our truck out though.

Everybody in Fairbanks bets on when breakup will come. For two bucks you can fill out a little card with the day, hour, minute, and second you think the ice will melt at a certain spot on the Tanana River. The person whose guess is closest gets thousands of dollars.

I don't win. But when breakup comes at the end of April, Len and I go out to a bulk store where people from the interior—Natives mostly—stock up for six months at a time. We load up on flour and sugar, bulgur and rice. We get cans of honey and of lard. We get dried fruit for vitamins until we have our own berries. We buy a couple of gallon jars of dried salmon until we can start getting our own fish. We throw in some canned sausages in case we get the craving for meat before Len can shoot a moose.

"I'll shoot a moose for food," he tells me. "But I don't want to catch anything in a trap, even there is good money for the fur. OK?"

"OK," I say.

X-Man stops by and tells us we need to pay up pretty soon. We are into our second month now and we still owe him for everything. X-Man says we'd better go ahead and pay up because he'd hate to have to take our truck. He would sure hate to have to do something like that. He says he's not cut out for business, that's his problem.

Len smiles and tells X-Man not to worry. He won't have to take our truck.

A few nights later the guy who owns the strip club tells me I should come out sometime and see how good his dancers have it. He's got a shortage of dancers right now, he says.

You can make a lot, he tells me. If you're good. If you're into it. If you've got the legs. It's more of a leg job than anything.

The girls make so much, they take trips to Hawaii every month, he says. They leave Fairbanks on the midnight flight and they're in Hawaii by seven in the morning.

"Who gets to go to Hawaii?" one of the girls with him says. It's the first thing I've heard either of them say, though they've both been in a few times. "*I* never got to go to Hawaii."

"If you tried a little harder you could so shut up," he tells her.

The girl reaches out and knocks over her drink on purpose. She'd had a sloe gin fizz so now everything is blood red. There's red splattered on the guy's white shirt.

He slaps her and knocks over *his* drink with his elbow. He grabs her and shakes her so her head kind of bobbles. He bangs her around so much that all the glasses and a plate of onion rings go crashing to the floor. The busboy runs over and starts sopping at the guy's shirt with a towel. I crawl under the table to pick the broken stuff up.

At about the same time I hear the girl finally start to cry, I see the guy's money clip lying on the carpet, the bills wet and pink. I manage to get ten or so out before I slide the clip back up onto the table. Both of the girls are crying now, but silently, their hand in their laps, their faces scrunched like babies.

"Some guy in the restaurant dropped his money clip," I whisper to Len that night when I get in bed. "I took out some bills, nine hundred dollars. He didn't notice because he was hitting a girl."

"Wow," Len whispers.

"Did you know you can fly to Hawaii in six hours," I say. "There's a flight every midnight. The hookers fly there every month. Supposedly."

Len tightens his arms around me.

"Do you want to fly to Hawaii?" he asks.

I think about the warm air and the warm water and the gleaming beach. I think about the girls lying in the sun, their bodies brown and oily, their faces behind sunglasses only a little beat-up.

"No," I say. "I want to go out to our land."

"Then," Len says. "Let's go."

We get up and get dressed. We don't light lanterns but we open the stove doors. In the low light, we pack our clothes and dishes and books and the supplies we have brought inside. We take down the shelves Len has put up and tie the boards together. At four we are all packed up; we get back in the bags and sleep for a few hours, then get up and stuff the sleeping bags and roll up the mattress. When X-Man's truck pulls away at nine, we knock the fire out of the stoves and break down the stovepipes. We load them in the truck. We take down the tent and load it. It's a tight fit, but we get the insulation and carpet in too. Len stands looking at the platform, but decides it will take too long to knock it apart and load it on top of the truck.

Before we leave, he takes off his California plates and wires on some Oregon plates he happens to have.

We fight the morning traffic out of town. But instead of heading up the Steese Highway, we get back on Highway 2 driving south.

"This isn't the way up to Circle," I say. "This is the way back down."

"We're not putting in at Circle," Len tells me. "We're putting in at Eagle. We have to drive down to Tok Junction and cut north."

He pulls over to the side of the road and gets out his map and a pencil. He erases the dot he showed X-Man and makes another dot on a little river that shoots off the Yukon.

Len smiles at me.

"Poor old X-Man," Len says. "He's really not cut out for business."